DEVILS

IN

THE CAVERN

Peter Wright

authorHOUSE®

AuthorHouse™ UK Ltd.
500 Avebury Boulevard
Central Milton Keynes, MK9 2BE
www.authorhouse.co.uk
Phone: 08001974150

First published by AuthorHouse 3/25/2010

ISBN: 978-1-4520-0462-4 (e)
ISBN: 978-1-4490-9858-2 (sc)

This book is printed on acid-free paper.

DEDICATION

To
Ruth; for her invaluable assistance as a sighted person which helped me enormously whenever I needed it. She's also my caring, loving and dedicated partner.

ACKNOWLEDGEMENT

Linda Callow; many thanks for the help and support she freely gave me.

PROLOGUE

1660. The hard ridden sounds of the horses hoof beats bore down on the quiet, small English village. Their riders held flaming torches, wearing swords at their sides. A horse-drawn cart, laden with poles of wood and bracken, followed closely behind. A tall, broad-shouldered man, wearing clothes of a better standard than those of his soldiers, shouted out his orders. He told his men to surround the village. He was the master, Lord of the land, high in peerage.

"I am Lord Carberry," he shouted as he entered the main square. "Bring out those responsible!"

The village remained silent, daring to confront his Lordship.

"Very well, you will all suffer. Burn the village, bring them to me!"

The men on horseback began setting fire to the thatched roofs. The villagers had no choice: come out into the open or be burned alive inside their own dwellings.

Swords were used to gather the villagers to the square. His Lordship produced a scrolled document, which would condemn the ringleaders.

"I, Lord Carberry, peer to the realm of King Charles

the Second, Knight of his Sovereign, do hereby decree that the village of 'Maple Leaf,' and its inhabitants, are hereby charged of witchcraft and heresy. The following names are to be found guilty of the fore-mentioned violations of our Sovereign, King Charles the Second. You will step forward unless you would rather see the whole village condemned: Joseph Hunt, John Dawson, Wilfred Burrowson and Matthew Townsend."

Struggles erupted as the crowd panicked and jostled with their loved ones. Women screamed with terror, children by their sides, shouting, "For heaven's sake … our children … think of our children."

The crowd started to settle down as a main ringleader, Matthew Townsend, stepped forward.

"I am he, known as Matthew Townsend. My family has nothing to do with this. Sir, I beg you, give them pardon."

"I will be the judge of these matters. Seize him!"

Matthew was taken to one side by the armed guards. One by one, the other three men came forward and begged forgiveness.

"You will each make your mark on this document, but be warned, those who do not confess, will see their families' suffer."

With no other choice, each man signed away his life.

"Good, very good. Take them to the stakes!" Lord Carberry ruled.

The whole village was ordered to go to the area where stakes had been erected by men in the cart. Located at one end of the village, four men were tied to individual stakes. Bracken was pulled from the cart and piled around their feet. By this time, the village was well alight with not a cottage spared.

"Step forward, you womenfolk of these men!" the ruthless Lord ordered. "Your menfolk are evil Satanists. You shall set thy torch to the death of them all. Be this a lesson in your lives before you all depart this place, never to return."

The howling women were forced by the Lord's guards to set fire to the bracken surrounding each man.

The bracken soon took hold and within minutes, the burning flesh filled the air with a repugnant stench.

One of the men, Matthew Townsend, who still had life left in him, cursed his Lordship. "Thou shalt see'eth thy inheritance in Satan's land. I await thee. Cursed be thy name."

The wailing villagers then listened to the harsh words of the laughing Lord Carberry. "Your curses mean nothing. I am a God-fearing man and I will protect His name in my lands, as I would protect our sovereign Lord, King Charles the Second! You villagers will now leave this place and go forward, out of the county of Lincolnshire."

Sobbing villagers were driven out. After they were gone and the burning was finished, his Lordship ordered the ash be put together and buried at the end of the village graveyard while the original graves of the churchyard be taken up, then re-interred, in other villages.

CHAPTER 1

1975.

Six months passed since Stan had shown a considerable interest in a girl he noticed while attending a graduation dance. An event that was organized by the university they both attended.

The most beautiful girl he had ever seen, Stan knew he had fallen in love with her. Irresistible and, even better, intelligent, this was made obvious by the fact that she had completed her second degree in psychology. Her first was a PhD in history.

Stan's achievements were also impressive, with a PhD in both architecture and civil engineering.

But, this girl enthralled him. She danced with such vigour. Her flowing, long, golden hair moved across her almost naked shoulders, save for two tiny straps. These held up a long, white gown, encrusted with gold layering around the seams.

Stan's friends could see that the interest was there, so they urged him on to go and dance with her.

"I don't even know her name," he tried to explain, but this was soon remedied.

"Charlotte," one of his friends said, "but she doesn't like being called that, so call her Charlie."

With some trepidation, Stan wandered over to where Charlotte was dancing, along with a group of her own friends.

"Hi, I'm Stan," he blurted out. "I wonder if you would do me the honour of dancing with me?"

Charlie's giggling friends moved from her side, giving them a chance to be alone. It turned out, however, that the one dance lasted all night long as they hit it off like a rocket being fired into outer space.

Within those first six months, Charlie's personality became more distinct. Considering her background-- brought up in a manor, having a knight of the realm for a father and a "lady of the manor" for a mother, she showed that really, she was just one of the gang. Charlie was a normal, happy-go-lucky young lady, without the "upper crust" type of personality that the genteel would have. This intrigued Stan, born as Stanley, since he was just a middle class, working man. There were no boundaries. They were destined to be together.

A lovely, full-mooned evening in the middle of spring found them holding hands in a beautiful park, simply strolling along, laughing and very much in love. It was the right time, Stan thought. He had to do it there and then.

Stopping Charlie in her tracks, he suddenly fell to one knee. The proposal came as no great shock to Charlie, but she couldn't help but smile when it happened.

"The answer," she confirmed, "is most definitely, yes. Of course I'll marry you. I love you so much, Stan."

He stood, drew her closer and kissed her passionately. Standing slightly back from her he fumbled with his jacket, producing a ring from the inside pocket. Contained inside a small blue box, cushioned in red satin. A ring of white gold with a large central diamond surrounded by small rubies, It fitted perfectly on the dainty third finger of Charlie's left hand and shone brightly, like a star sent from heaven.

Stan took her in his arms and lifted her up into the air. Smiling, laughing in fact, she nearly cried with joy and happiness.

At this very moment a passing couple, much older in years, stopped and clapped them. Privileged to have witnessed this most wonderful moment that couldn't have been any more romantic, the old couple would, most likely, cherish this for a very long time. After all, it wasn't very often that this sort of scene confronted them.

"How simply wonderful!" the white haired old lady commented. "We hope you'll both be as happy as we are."

Stan and Charlie thanked them with kisses for their kind words. The scene captured a moment in time, making not only the future bride and groom happy, but the two old folks as well.

Stan decided they should celebrate with a drink at their local.

Charlie agreed and skipped along without a care in the world. They eventually came to the riverside hotel, a typical old English building with beams of black oak standing proudly amongst the white walls. It seemed to be an ideal place; romantic and charming.

Looking around the dimly lit room, a few local friends were already chatting and drinking.

"Best not to say anything to them," whispered Stan holding Charlie's hand and being careful not to bang his head on the low beamed ceiling. "Your mother and father should be the first to know."

"Agreed," said Charlie looking as bright as her yellow knee length dress, "but I'll take the ring off, so Papa and Momma can see it first."

The couple sat down and toasted their friends and colleagues, but their happiness was evident, which made them appear a little more than suspicious. One even commented on how radiant Charlie looked, as if there was a big secret.

"Seems like you two are holding back on something, not getting married are you?" the young man asked. But the secret, although they were bursting to tell them, was safe… for the time being, anyway.

Their friends didn't stay very long, as it happened, because they were off to the town's nightclubs. Although they did ask Stan and Charlie to go with them, they declined, wanting to be alone.

Stan looked at Charlie with a calm expression of love and affection. Mixed thoughts ran through his mind. Stan wanted to be honest with her. He didn't want any secrets between them. No surprises and certainly no skeletons in the closet that could harm their beautiful relationship.

"Charlie, if we are to have a good honest relationship, then it's important that there should be nothing in our lives that could possibly harm us. I need to tell you a little of my past. It's something I feel strongly about. I hope you feel the same way."

"Well, okay then, I think. You're right, Stan. I hope it's not too serious?" She looked a little concerned.

"Well, no, I don't think so. It's nothing to worry about, I assure you." He held her hands lovingly across the table." It's okay darling, really," he reassured her. "Do you remember when I told you that I only went out with one other girl in my life?"

"Yes, but I wasn't very interested. It was well before you had even met me."

"Well, I just think that it's best to be open and honest with each other."

She looked in his eyes moving her hand to caress his face. "I'm sorry, Stan. I should listen a bit more. It is important to me as well, please do tell."

Stan trembled slightly, looking down at his drink. "It's a few years back now, but I was going out with a girl named "Irene.""

Pausing for a while, re-living the nightmare of that one dreaded night in Australia's outback region. He recalled how Irene had gone missing while on a survey of the outback's roads.

She was a brilliant young biologist, who had a good career in front of her. He remembered that day very well, so well that he even had nightmares.

She had gone out into the bush to study the wild life, ignoring Stan's concern about how dangerous it could be to go out into the bush at nighttime. No one could stop this wild young vixen from doing what she liked, that's the way it was with her. Although she promised him she would not stray too far from their encampment, even so, he worried about her. He explained to her that he was working on a tight schedule on his particular section of the survey and it needed to be completed on time or else he would have gone with her.

Unfortunately, she never returned.

"I tell you Charlie, I searched for hours, but there was no sign of her anywhere." Once again, he paused as Charlie gently moved her hand up and down Stan's quivering arm. 'It's fine darling, take your time,' she persuaded him.

He recalled contacting the police, sobbing while waiting. A helicopter arrived, put down a police officer then the helicopter did a search. A massive manhunt began. The only thing they found, after many days, was one of her shoes by the side of a river.

The police trackers could only surmise that she had either fallen into the river and could not get out, or that one of the many crocodiles had pounced on her. Either way, no remains, or body, were ever found. After some six months of searching the area, the authorities pronounced her missing and presumed dead. Stan finally gave up his own search and returned to England, but not before much interrogation by the police.

Charlie felt sorry for Stan. All she could do was console him, but Stan told her that while he could never forget his past, he knew he had to move on with his life. After all, Irene had disappeared five years ago.

Charlie thought Stan was very brave in coping with such a trauma, but the past, after all, was the past.

"I don't have a past like that, Stan, but I'll tell you what I can about my own history." Charlie related her own uneventful story of being brought up in her upper class environment. She explained that she never really bothered with all the pomp and circumstance. In fact, she was thought of as being an odd one out, being more of a tomboy, always wearing jeans and being a little rough with her playmates, and even the residential staff. Her mother wanted her to be more of a lady, but her dresses often got torn or stained, due to her roguish behaviour.

Basically, she would do what she wanted. Her father admired her individuality with resigned reflection. He actually wished he could be more like her, a free soul, fighting her own fights and making her own decisions to suit her own lifestyle.

When it came down to it though, she knew she was the only child, brought up in a world of privilege. This only inspired her to take some liberties, although not taking too much advantage of her own position. She certainly did not go as far as to make fools of her parents. No, she loved them too much for that. After all, they were all very open and freely gave their own opinions. And because of this, her pet names for her parents were, 'Papa' and 'Momma'.

"It's really rather funny, you know, Stan. I was christened with the name Charlotte, but when I was about five years old, I decided I would be called Charlie. And, I made sure my parents understood this. They thought I had developed a 'wild side' in me, which they found amusing at that age. I always insisted they call me Charlie because I thought Charlotte was just too pompous."

Stan laughed as Charlie leaned forward and giggled. "Yes, I can well believe that. Do you think we could, well, for the moment anyway, move away from all of this? It's just that I realize I will have to ask your father's permission for your hand in marriage. The thought of it makes me feel nervous."

"Oh, you are so sweet. Do I detect a hint of old fashioned values here?"

"Er, uh, well, I just thought it was the right thing to do. Don't you agree then?"

"Don't you worry. I'm only having you on. I think it's sweet, romantic and the sort of thing papa would insist upon in any case. Tell you what, I know that both my parents will be in the day after tomorrow, so I'll see what I can do, okay?"

Stan had met her parents on a number of occasions, although usually briefly, but he already knew they were quite taken with him.

Charlie also knew her father was particularly taken with Stan, believing him to be quite the gentleman, in fact. He seemed to have the good morals of the old-fashioned principles, which would serve him well.

As usual, Stan took Charlie back to her flat, where she had been living as a student. With their student days finally over, tomorrow Charlie would return to her family home, White Haven Hall. They would not see each other until Stan came to officially break the news to her parents. She agreed to telephone him with the arrangements.

The big day soon arrived for Stan to make the journey to Oxford. Feeling rather nervous, yet content and happy, eagerly he drove through the long, country roads, admiring the splendid views.

A large wall surrounded the grounds of the hall with two double, cast iron gates at the entrance. An intercom fastened to the gates was part of the security features. Stan got out of his car and pushed the button. "Er, hello, I'm Stanley Harrow. Can anyone hear me?"

A quiet, well-spoken voice suddenly erupted from the external loudspeaker. "Yes sir, I hear you. You are expected sir. Please follow the road to the hall, where you will find the main doorway."

The gates opened automatically, with a sudden urgency to spur him on. As he drove along the tree-lined road, he could see the magnificent White Haven Hall, a spectacle that made him wince with fear.

A well-dressed gentleman, charming and polite-- probably the butler, he imagined, welcomed Stan into the foyer. Charlie had spotted Stan's car coming up the driveway, so decided to rush down the double winding staircase that stood proudly in the middle of the foyer with its magnificent balustrades, once used as her playground.

"Shall I take your coat, sir?"

Before he knew it, Charlie was on Stan like a flash, kissing him quickly.

"I'll get it," she told the butler. "Oh Stan, I've missed you!"

She gently pulled Stan's overcoat from him, handing it to the surprised butler and guided Stan to the library, where her parents were seated, reading. They stood, then immediately greeted Stan like he was already a member of the family. Incessant chatter erupted as various subjects, mostly about university life and their successes were covered. Stan's eyes were aghast at the sight of thousands of books that filled the large room. The dark oak table, some fifteen feet in length was surrounded by several leather-upholstered chairs. After about twenty minutes, the butler came into the room and announced that lunch was being served.

Charlie guided Stan into the dining room behind her parents, which was the formal thing to do.

"You sit here Stan, next to me," Charlie insisted, before he could utter a word.

Seated amidst a wonderful display of well-presented foods, which were presented on the whitest of white linen that draped a long table, two maids, ornate with pristine black and white outfits, stood patiently. Their hands were clasped gently in front of them as they waited to help serve the delicious foods.

The butler busied himself with the seating of the lord and lady, then presented the white wine vintage 1940 Chablis, for his lordship's approval.

"Excellent choice, James. Excellent!"

With the approval of the Chablis, James gave a quick nod to the waiting maids, who quickly and efficiently served Stan and Charlie the wine.

Stan seemed a little over-awed by the attention he received from one of the maids., a pretty auburn haired girl, about twenty years old. She knew her manners, as well as her efficient knowledge of serving the guests. When their work was completed, the maids resumed their position by the tapestry-laden wall. Here they stayed until summoned.

The meal proceeded with smiling faces and a cheerful atmosphere. Charlie couldn't help herself by teasing Stan a little. A few winks made him blush with embarrassment, which made her giggle like a small child. At the end of the meal, she started to squeeze his leg under the table, whispering, "Now Stan, now."

"I believe Stan would like to talk to you, Papa," she insisted.

Finally, with attention drawn towards Stan, he plucked up the courage to address his lordship. "I would like to talk to you, Sir, if I may?"

"What, what? Oh, yes, of course, my lad. Would you prefer some privacy?"

"Yes sir, if you don't mind."

"Come then. We will go into the lounge."

Some twenty minutes later, the two men re-emerged to join Charlie and her mother.

"Looks like we have a marriage to arrange, Mildred, " His lordship happily spoke, "I have given my permission for this young man to wed our daughter." He smiled while looking at Stan.

A sudden gust of excitement swept over not only Charlie's face, but her mother as well. His lordship summoned James by pulling a cord situated by an open fire, to bring the best champagne he could find in the cellar.

"Well, I think that since you are going to be my son-in-law, it would be more appropriate to call me George. Well then, what about you Mildred?"

"Goodness, yes, please call me Mildred. It is much better, Stanley."

"Thank you sir, er, I mean George." Stan looked at Charlie's mother, "Thanks Mildred."

A party of champagne then ensued with great joy.

The two women soon got their heads together, sitting in armchairs close to the log fire, organising and planning their options of how the wedding should proceed, even coming up with a date for the event.

CHAPTER 2

His lordship, MBE OBE, as well as an MP for Grantham, spent a fair time at his ancestral home, "Carberry Manor", a large mansion that was bombed by the Germans in the Second World War. It lay somewhat derelict for nearly twenty years. Since that period, George decided to rebuild and restore this once luxurious manor to its former glory. The restoration was now nearing completion, which was good news for George, because over the years he had spent many millions of pounds on the project.

Although his wife, Mildred supported and indeed had a great influence on its restoration, they never told Charlie of its existence, because it was to be a surprise inheritance for her. She only knew that Papa always seemed to be away at the Commons or elsewhere on business. She didn't really mind this too much though because, after all, it gave her the opportunity to be more of a free agent.

A month before the wedding, George invited Stan over to lunch. Casual dress would be fine, Stan was informed. George told Stan they would discuss the final plans of the wedding.

Charlie couldn't resist playing a joke on her parents, especially when they specified the type of dress code. Casual to them meant smart casual, while dinner dress was suits and evening wear; usually ball gown for the ladies. The urge to embarrass her parents was overwhelming, cheeky in fact, but nevertheless, very humorous. Dressing in the complete opposite of what they wanted would cause raised eyebrows when she walked in on a dinner party wearing casual clothing. A lot of the time though, she wore jeans, then told everyone that she thought it was casual wear. There would be a lot of laughter, as her mother would call out, "Oh Charlie, it's evening dress, dear."

Because of this, it came as no surprise, therefore, to find that when Stan arrived at the mansion, he was greeted by his beautifully dressed fiancée, in evening wear. His own appearance showed that while he dressed in trousers and jacket, he certainly didn't come up to Charlie's standard.

"Oh my God," he gasped, "I thought this was a casual affair, have I made a mistake? You look absolutely stunning!"

"Of course it is … I just thought it would be a bit of a laugh. You watch their faces when I walk in, they won't know what to do. I'm hoping that they'll think they have got it wrong."

"Well, thank God for that! You certainly got me going, that's for sure. What will I do with you?" Stan said as he relaxed and hugged Charlie.

She giggled as she took him by his hand. Leading him straight to the sitting room, where her parents were waiting. The look on Charlie's face, as she glanced towards her parents was a picture indeed. Both George and Mildred were standing by the log fire, wearing their best evening attire. George wore his grey suit, dicky bow and top hat, while Mildred was adorned in a top-of-the-range gown, along with a diamond necklace and tiara, encrusted with a mixture of diamonds and other precious stones.

"A bit surprised, my dear? We rather thought that you might try to embarrass us, but we know you a little better than that," grinned George!

Charlie was speechless, Stan started to laugh, then Mildred and finally, George.

"Mildred? Have, you got the camera handy?" remarked George as he held out his arm looking rather smug.

"Don't you dare, Papa. Okay, you got me. I'm going to have to be a bit more careful in the future, by the looks of it!"

"Come on in, Stanley," Mildred laughed, holding her stomach with the pains of laughing. "You'll have to forgive us, but I'm afraid we could not resist getting our own back on Charlotte! Rather funny, don't you think?"

"I don't think she knew what to do, when she saw you both like that, but it was funny. I think it's great to see that you all have a good sense of humour, madam."

"It was a first for us, Stanley, remarked Mildred, "just to see her face. Now then George, perhaps we can go and get changed into something a bit more comfortable!"

George and Mildred, still laughing, walked out of the room, kissing their red-faced daughter as they went.

"Looks like they got their own back on you Charlie," laughed Stan pulling one of the chairs closer so they could be sat next to each other. Stan remarked on the wonderful job the decorators had made, preserving its old features. The overhanging crystal chandeliers sparkled brightly over the lower set coffee tables. A large tiger rug, complete with a large head, lay on the maple floorboards while another lamb's wool rug, lay close to the hearth. Spears of African origin decorated a most colourful, 'Zulu' shield hanging on one wall.

By the time that Charlie's parents re-entered the room, the atmosphere was now one of complete relaxation. James, the butler, came into the room and announced, "Luncheon is now ready".

They all moved into the dining room where a wonderful spread of salmon, several meats, spiced chicken and all manner of assorted salad greens and dips, were laid out before them. The maids were busy bringing them fresh prawn cocktails as a starter, while others were laying out different types of dessert on a large trolley. Drinks were served in the usual way.

"Will that be all, sir?" asked James pouring his masters drink.

"Thank you, James, a lovely spread, as always. My compliments to cookie."

After dinner, they all moved into the lounge, where his lordship stood and announced that he had something to tell the young couple. Mildred joined her husband by his side.

"We would like to give you a wedding present, your mother and I. One that will start you off in the right direction in your lives." He produced a set of keys, from his pocket. "These keys are to a cottage in Lincolnshire. We thought you would need a home to start your new life together."

With tears running down her face, Charlie stood and ran to them, giving both a big hug. "Oh Papa, Momma, I love you both so much. This is wonderful. Thank you."

Stan also got up, then thanked them profusely.

After being handed the deed to the home, they were told that there was some land attached to the property, which might inspire them. Also, they would find a very nice old fashioned, country village called Little Leaf just down the road. This was extremely wonderful news to Charlie and Stan, with much celebration taking place the remainder of the night.

CHAPTER 3

A few days later, Stan and Charlie decided to visit the cottage, to see what decorating or repairs the home might need. Situated in a small village, just as they had been told, the place was peaceful and idyllic; it lay about five miles east of Grantham.

There couldn't have been many more than a dozen small cottages in the village as they drove through, they noticed a single church, one small shop and a public house called, Maple Lodge. Time seemed to have stood still here. Horses and carts were still being used like they were a century ago. This place, well off the beaten track, was surrounded by hawthorn hedges that separated crops of corn, wheat and an odd tree known for its many years of age.

At the end of the village stood the two-story, thatched cottage. Much bigger than the others in the village, the cottage boasted of five bedrooms, two bathrooms, a large lounge and a dining room. A small study, with its picturesque fireplace, seemed ideal for its purpose. The kitchen, although antique in appearance, included a fine, black, cast iron range, along with a copper clad hood that ascended the stone-faced wall. This beautiful kitchen would certainly give plenty of scope, as well as room, to any good adventurous cook.

Outside, sixty acres of good, prime farmland were interrupted by a larger than normal, spinney of maple trees.

"It's strange, you know, Stan," Charlie suggested, "maybe this is the place where the village derived its name from. Look at the small leaves on the maple trees. Little leaves, or should I say, Little Leaf."

"You may well be right, my princess," Stan said, his powerful arms enveloping her small waist, "it seems romantically suitable."

The low ceiling, prevalent throughout the cottage with its blackened oak beams, brought a certain romance to Charlie. While they explored the bedrooms and without a word of warning, she threw herself into his arms and kissed him passionately. She felt a little more than ecstatic. She was in Heaven and tearing at his clothes.

Stan couldn't believe what she was doing as he told her to slow down. He felt very lucky and extremely fortunate to have this beautiful girl, as well as a beautiful cottage.

A sudden banging at the front door, however, stopped them dead in their tracks.

"Oh flipping heck!" Charlie moaned. "Typical, just typical. Who on earth could that be?"

Straightening themselves out, Charlie made her way to the front door.

"Morning miss, my name is Cartwright, and this is Mrs Cartwright. We're your house keeper and farm manager."

Pausing for a moment, the well-groomed gent, in a

brown tweed jacket, cloth cap and well pressed matching trousers, looked every bit the squire's gentleman.

"Sorry to disturb you, but when we saw you come to the cottage, we thought we'd introduce ourselves. You'll be seeing quite a lot of us, but we won't stay. We know you've just come to view the old place, so we'll make tracks and see you soon."

"No, don't go, "Charlie politely begged. "Please, do come in. This is a bit of a surprise to me. I had no idea." Extending a hand towards Stan, she added, "This is my future husband, Stan."

Stan greeted them with a handshake, then stared at them.

"Sorry, I'm Bill and this is Edna, sir. Pleasure indeed madam, sir."

They walked silently into the cottage. Stan gazed at Charlie wondering who these people really were.

"I don't think that we know anything about this, do we, Charlie?" asked Stan.

"No, I didn't Stan."

"Oh, sorry about that, ma'am. Your father has employed us for many years now. We are at your disposal."

Questioning the couple, Charlie wondered why they needed a farm manager.

The strange glance that occupied this shrewd character made Stan study him with some concern. "Well, let's just say," compelled Mr Cartwright, "ma'am, that your father owns a lot more than just this small part here. I can't say much more than that. Your father has given me strict instructions to say no more. Sorry, ma'am, sir."

Accepting this explanation with some intrigue, Bill and Edna were welcomed.

The Cartwrights had, by now, already started towards the front door, apologizing for disturbing the young couple as they went.

"I'll get the workmen in for you," Bill added. "I dare say a lick of paint is in order. Just leave instructions and I'll see that it gets done. Cheerio for now."

"Strange people," said Stan, "but I think we may need that housekeeper. This place is rather larger than I thought. I don't quite understand though, why on earth would we need a farm manager? I wouldn't have thought the farm was big enough."

"Well, sweet lover," Charlie remarked with her own interpretation, hands on her hips, "I expect its probably just a title for someone to look after the land. You know, keep it in order, count the sheep, or something like that."

"It's still a bit strange though, don't you think?" as Stan stroked his chin.

"Well I'll just have to ask Papa. I'm sure there's more to this than what we're being told. But, I can't understand what the big secret is? How much land does Papa actually own?" She shook her head, peering through the windows at the great expanse of their land. "I don't really understand all of this."

The bemused couple continued with their survey, then headed back home.

CHAPTER 4

When Charlie eventually arrived home, she found the mansion quite deserted, apart from the butler and maids. She asked James if Papa was home, but he told her that he had had to go back to the Commons.

"Your mother, miss, has gone to London. She will be back in one week."

This was nothing unusual. Work often took the Carberrys away on business, for weeks at times. A phone call from her mother soon put Charlie's mind to rest. She told Charlie that a fitting for the wedding dress had been arranged and that it would take place at the manor, very soon.

A delighted Charlie, though, could only think about what the farm manager had said about the other land Papa owned near the village of Little Leaf, as well as the cleaner and farm manager.

"There's no need to concern yourself with a bit of land or the staff he employs. Heaven knows, I don't think that he does either, " said Mildred. "We own several sites around the country. Look, Charlie, I think we have enough to do organizing the wedding, let alone the business of land."

Charlie agreed with her mother because her mother was usually right in these matters.

Time sped by, what with the fitting of the wedding gown, the bridesmaids' outfits, cars, flowers and catering. This also included the making of a wedding cake, which was a speciality by their own cook.

Many different professional people visited the manor for various reasons, but mainly with things having to do with the wedding. This gave Charlie the impression that the place resembled that of a busy bee's nest.

Then, the big day finally came.

The maids and hairdresser all helped delightful Charlie get ready. Stan, on the other hand, still suffered from a mild hangover from the night before. He was fortunate to have the help of his best man.

A lot of activity was present in the main hall, better known as "the long room". This was a particularly lovely room, designed for banquets, conferences, dances and anything else that needed a lot of space.

At twelve thirty, the arrival of an old fashioned, white, Rolls Royce seemed to cause a little panic with Charlie's father, George. He could only be described as a headless chicken, running around in circles. Mildred, however, soon got him organized. Once they were in the cars, George settled down. He looked at Charlie with love and admiration, fussing around her, checking if everything was in order.

"My God, Charlotte," he mumbled, "you are the most beautiful young lady a father could ever hope to have. Simply stunning. I'm very proud of you."

A little trickle of tears ran down his face.

"Oh papa, don't cry, you'll have me doing it too, then my make-up will be ruined."

When the father and bride came into the lovely Grantham Cathedral, Stan gasped at the sight he beheld. He couldn't have ever imagined such a sight would make render him trembling with emotion. The beautiful bride was wearing the most exquisite wedding dress and a long, trailing train, being held up by four lovely bridesmaids.

The ceremony went very smoothly, no real problems, which was a relief for George. Mildred held a handkerchief to her eyes though. After the register had been signed, the beautiful voices of the cathedral's choir filled the air with a melodious rapture.

Two photographers were on hand to capture every possible scene. Lords, ladies, friends, in fact anyone worth knowing was present. This, in itself, presented headaches for the many stewards who were there, but they were well trained and very organized.

Back at the manor, however, the last ditch preparations were being made. The flower displays were having their positions meticulously altered, while the silver cutlery shone like mirrors against the purity of the silk tablecloths.

Stan and Charlie finally arrived at the manor. They could not have been more surprised at the formal yet awe-inspiring display of the glorious long room. Stan in particular was amazed with the transformation of such a large hall.

Soon, they were greeting guests, who were then promptly given a glass of champagne by the waiting maids. The many dignitaries, relatives and friends were shown their sitting positions. Calligraphically written place names added a classical touch.

Every table was soon filled with the chattering guests, as the best man gave the first of many toasts. The traditional cutting of the cake followed a five-course dinner. Dozens of telegrams and best wishes to the happy couple were read out amongst sighs and gasps.

Dancing ensued with happy and content people, to a ten-piece band.

The following day Stanley and Charlotte Harrow departed for their two-week honeymoon in Barbados.

CHAPTER 5

Having returned from their romantic honeymoon, Stan and Charlie soon accustomed themselves to a normal married life in their new home. Stan had, by now, been given some lucrative contracts, thanks to George and the many contacts he knew, which meant he had to work away from home for many days at a time.

Charlie didn't really need to work much, since they were pretty well off, as far as money was concerned, but she took up the position of a part-time administrator at a solicitor's office.

One day, whilst walking back through the village on a sun-drenched afternoon, she started thinking more about the cottage. She wasn't altogether satisfied with the layout of the rooms. She had already made several changes, mainly the decor, but was still not completely satisfied.

To her, there seemed to be an urge, if not a powerful force that was trying to reach out to her. She often thought that the house was, in some strange way, trying to talk to her. Even her dreams were being taken over by the cottage. Some of the dreams, however, turned out to be horrible nightmares, but others showed how the cottage used to look, before some extensive modernization had taken place.

This type of dream used to almost put Charlie into a sort of daydream trance and so, very often, she would make small changes. The latest idea that came to her involved knocking down a wall to create a larger living area. For this, though, she would need to consult Stan. He would be able to use his knowledge and expertise to see if this was plausible.

Charlie wasn't very sure whether Stan would agree with her anyway. He tended to be away lately on business, sometimes even out of the country. Nevertheless, Charlie phoned him to ask his opinion, but he told her to wait until he got home in two or three days.

That night, as she was reading a local history book of the area, she came across a story about her present house. Apparently, the house was built in the middle of an ancient graveyard, although there were no signs to indicate that it ever was. But this news certainly made her shiver just a little bit.

Reference was also made to the past tenants and, in particular, a man named Jack, who had disappeared under strange circumstances.

Yawning, Charlie was by now feeling very tired and put the book down for the evening.

Later that night, at about two o'clock in the morning, Charlie woke up, feeling very hot with perspiration. She had just had a bad dream about her own cottage. It seemed very spooky because of the strange things that were going on.

Jumping up out of her bed, she went downstairs for

a drink. As she got to the bottom of the stairs, a chill caressed her naked legs. A rather sudden, spine-chilling sensation, swept over her.

As she went through the lounge, the whole atmosphere seemed different. Apprehension dawned on her. It was as if there was somebody in the room, watching her every move.

She even shouted out, "Who's there?" but thesilence emanated from all around.

Finding the light switch soon put her at ease. It was quiet, too quiet in fact although it felt a bit weird.

Charlie, thinking she was being a bit silly, tried to put these thoughts out of her mind. After getting a glass of water from the kitchen, she went back through the lounge to check once more. She happened to touch one of the walls and was surprised to get an electric shock from it.

Knowing there were no electric sockets or switches located on this particular wall, she trembled with fright. A slight sense of panic ran through Charlie as she almost darted back to her bedroom. She lay in bed, cuddled up to her favourite teddy, but she soon found that she could not sleep very well.

The following day, she called in an electrician to check out the wiring in the whole house, just in case there was some kind of problem.

"Nothing wrong with the wiring ma'am, can't understand it at all," the bewildered electrician told her. Putting his hand on the wall, he continued, "Maybe it was just static electricity. These places tend to be full of it."

Charlie nodded her head in agreement. His thoughts sounded very logical.

The last couple of nights had made her feel so uneasy that it wasn't any wonder she couldn't wait for Stan to come home. Trying to keep busy, the thought finally occurred to her that this was the same wall she wanted to knock down, as part of her plans.

Stan arrived late in the afternoon, but was surprised to gain so many hugs and kisses from Charlie. She had certainly missed him. She made their dinner, then sat, talking about his work and also about what had been going on in the cottage.

They were still talking late into the evening, when they both remarked on how it had suddenly gone cold.

"Oh my gosh, it's happening again!" cried Charlie.

Stan got up and touched the wall. Immediately, he received a stunning jolt, which sent him reeling to the floor. He sat up, none the worse for wear.

"I think you may be right," he cursed, as he picked himself up. "It does seem to be alive, somehow."

The wall started to glow and tremble, then it seemed as if a doorway appeared. A greenish, yellow mist emanated from this doorway. Stan jumped back in surprise. "What the hell is going on here?" he cursed.

They were very tempted to go closer, although Stan was very wary, even extremely cautious of venturing too near, but Charlie, being who she was, went closer anyway and stood in front of it.

"Maybe this is how Jack disappeared." She queried.

"Jack? Oh the one in your book you mean.

Don't be ridiculous, Charlie. How can a man disappear through a wall?"

"Well, how do you explain what's happening now?" she retorted.

"I'm not altogether sure," Stan pressed, "but this isn't right, it just can't be happening."

As they pondered what they should do, a faint voice called out from the glowing doorway.

"Help me, please someone help me!"

They stood there, astounded, looking at each other. "There's someone in there!" they both said together.

Stan thought how ridiculous this all seemed, but Charlie knew she had to do something.

"Hold my hand, Stan. I want to get nearer to see what happens."

"For God's sake, Charlie, be careful, we don't know what may happen!"

"It's okay, Stan, but if someone is trapped, we have to find out more."

Cautiously, she lengthened her arm out and touched the quivering wall. It went straight through. At the same time though, she felt something, or someone, grab hold of her hand and, with a sudden almighty force, she was dragged in. Stan lost his grip on Charlie. He had not foreseen the danger that lurked there. How could he possibly know? He tumbled to the floor, dazed and confused. At this point, the quivering doorway suddenly closed up before Stan could gather any momentum to go forward. In a panic, he hit out at the wall, but got an almighty shock in return. His body shuddered, sending him sprawling, yet again, to the ground.

"Oh my God, Charlie, Charlie!" he shouted in vain, but it was no good. Charlie was gone.

CHAPTER 6

Stan sat up, wondering what the hell had gone on. There seemed little he could do as his thoughts drifted all over the place. Maybe there are secret switches hidden somewhere, but nothing seemed to be obvious. This thought didn't stop him from looking though. He couldn't comprehend that all of this was beyond him; something paranormal, sinister, maybe not of this earth. Remembering Irene and the awful nightmares he had gone through, he felt desperate that he may lose his dearest Charlie. Clasping his hands over his face, sitting on a chair, he refused to accept this situation, trying to be positive, not knowing what to do.

But then he remembered Charlie had been reading a book, something to do with the history of the area. Rushing upstairs, he soon found it. The book was on her bedside cabinet. Borrowed from the library, the pages told about the local history of the area during the 17th to 19th century. It seemed an appropriate book to read, since the house was built in 1803. Upon thumbing through the pages, Stan soon learned the site upon which the house had been built was on an ancient graveyard. According to the book, the village that existed at the time was burnt down, by order of the lord of the manor because of its involvement in sorcery and witchcraft.

The 17th century was a particular period of this kind of evilness. Severe punishment was handed out to anyone involved. These so-called, "pagans" dabbled in the dark arts. There was talk of sacrifices of innocent victims and grotesque sexual deviations.

The village, then known as Maplewood had its own village church and graveyard, which were also used in vile desecration. It was, to this end, that the entire area had been completely demolished and its inhabitants banished.

The graveyard, small as it was at that time, was dug up and moved to a neighbouring village, or so it was thought.

In 1750, when the village was renamed Little Leaf, the then lord, of Carberry Manor, who had inherited the manor from his grandfather, arrived on the scene. Immediately, he ordered a new village to be built for the workers on his estate.

Strict rules burdened what the new villagers could do in and around their homes, and on the land. A small church was built and everyone was expected to attend. To make sure Lord Carberry always attended. Notes of those who didn't attend were made, and a good reason was necessary by those few as to why they had been absent. These people would receive a visit from the God-fearing lord, who would impose fines. These were often very heavy, so a good attendance always seemed to exist.

In 1803, the last house that was ever built in the village had, inadvertently, been built on the old site of the graveyard. Many rumours evolved after its construction. Some of the craftsmen fell mysteriously ill, while another lost his life.

Although the work was completed, no one would occupy the dwelling for many years. This was due to a local farm worker who was walking past the house when he saw strange, greenish lights and sounds. These sounds, he reported, "Were from the devil himself." He also spoke of a strange mist that radiated from all around the dwelling. The villagers soon learned of these mysterious events, which only served to produce even more rumours. Potential tenants were soon scared off by these allegations, so Lord Carberry had the house sealed up. It wasn't until 1815 that the house was finally occupied.

In 1942, a man known as Jack Beaumont suddenly vanished without a trace and the police never found any clues. His belongings, even a cupboard of fresh food, were still present but his body was nowhere to be found.

Charlie underlined the last paragraph Stan read. For what reason, he wasn't sure. Yes, she had briefly mentioned Jacks name, but that was about all. He could only imagine that some sort of link was possible. She must have done this to bring attention to this man, Jack Beaumont.

No obvious clues were present, except several papers that told of the black arts, witchcraft and devilry. He ignored these, threw them on the floor and went back downstairs.

Franticly, he ran his hands over the wall for a reaction, but nothing happened. In fact, everything appeared quite normal.

He knew he needed some sort of help, but who would

believe him even if he could find someone? The only people he could think of were the local police department. Without hesitation, although panicking like a mad man, he eventually found his keys to the car, jumped in, then drove himself to the police station.

The sergeant on the desk listened to Stan's story, but he could only just about stop himself from laughing.

"Let's get this right, sir. You are trying to tell me that your wife walked up to this wall and, while holding her hand, she got pulled in, then vanished?" the sergeant sniggered.

"Yes, that's exactly the way it was!" blurted out frustrated Stan.

"You haven't been drinking, have you, sir?"

"How dare you, sergeant. I am telling you the truth."

"All right then sir, calm down. Would you like to report a missing person?"

"My God," he whimpered, "you don't believe a word I've said, do you sergeant?"

Stan knew he wouldn't get anywhere like this, especially with this sort of attitude. He did, however, give his wife's details. He then walked out, feeling a lot worse than when he first went in.

Once Stan departed the police station, the sergeant could not stop laughing and called his colleagues to have them listen to his story. They, too, could not believe such a wild tale like this. Soon, the whole station heard of the story amidst great howls of laughter.

CHAPTER 7

Feeling disillusioned by the police, Stan drove back home wondering what to do next as he continued to struggle coming to terms with this problem. Arriving back home, he wandered back upstairs, but not before first examining the dreaded wall. He picked up the book and flipped through the pages. He realized that the only person that could possibly help him would be some sort of spiritualist medium.

Without delay he set to work researching phone books and his contact list to find a suitable person. This took many hours, but Stan would not give up, he would search all night if necessary. He was quite surprised to discover that a medium actually lived in the village. He wasted no time in trying to contact this person, known locally as "Gentle Jim". He soon found himself within the village, knocking on doors.

"Oh yes, you mean Gentle Jim," one of the villagers told him. "You'll find him at number six. It's just across the road."

Thanking the pleasant man, Stan ran furiously across the cobbled road. He soon found the cottage and knocked on the door.

Gentle Jim stood six feet five inches tall, sporting a well-grown, dark beard and had very broad shoulders. He answered the door as Stan hurriedly blurted out his mixed-up story.

"Whoa, slow down," Jim hastily retorted. "Come inside and tell me properly."

After sitting Stan down and offering him a tot of whisky, Jim listened with amazement at the strange story Stan, who by now seemed a little calmer, relayed to him.

They talked for many hours while sipping tea, but Jim came to the conclusion that he would come to the house with Stan that night, in order to start an investigation.

It was ten o'clock when they eventually turned up at the cottage. Immediately, Jim went into his mediumistic ways.

"I need to walk around the house first Stan, to see what I can pick up." The giant gently confirmed.

Stan stood quietly, feeling nervous, the anticipation showing in his face. It didn't take too long, however, for Jim to complete his tour and return to the lounge. He told Stan that whatever was here was most certainly in this room.

"There seems to be some residual energy here but I have grave feelings for this place, there's something not quite right. I am picking up on some sort of dark entity. It seems to be hiding in the shadows."

"I don't understand Jim," panicked Stan, "I know nothing of these residual energies, entities or shadows you talk about. What are they?"

It took a few minutes to explain to Stan the terms Jim used. Apparently, the residual energy was the energy that was left behind in the fabric of the building, a sort of recording of past individuals. The entities, he explained, were an unknown phenomena, mainly because it was sometimes difficult to tell whether it was in human shape or animal form, or a mixture of both. "The latter," he explained, "had no identifiable shape to mere mortals. It came from the dark realms, satanic ghouls, one might say." Jim continued to explain about the significance of the shadows. "This means that entities are simply keeping out of sight. "They don't want to be seen by anyone, let alone a good medium. So basically, they hide."

Jim then went back to work, concentrating and moving slowly around the room. He called out to the dark entity, but was driven back with a great force of power. He ended up falling to the floor, writhing in agony.

"My leg," he groaned, "Jesus, it got me! Come and check out my leg!"

Stan rushed to his side and noticed blood running down his right leg. He pulled up the bloodied trouser leg and saw what looked like a gruesome gash, some five inches long, across the back of his leg.

"My God! What the hell did that? I didn't even see anything."

"It's okay, Stan. It's not as bad as it looks."

Stan helped Jim to a chair then quickly rushed off to the kitchen to find a suitable dressing. He soon stopped the flow of blood then applied a bandage.

"What the heck is going on, Jim? I never saw anything in this room move. How did you get this wound? What sort of creature could do this?"

"Calm down, Stan. I've seen this sort of thing before.

Don't worry. I'll put some protection on us. It seems though, there's more to this than meets the eye. I've discovered a portal. Trouble is, it seems to come and go. Normally, they stay in one place, but this one seems to be able to open and close on command. It's like an escape route, but for whatever purpose, I don't yet understand. It seems to be a bit of a mystery."

"What the heck is a portal, Jim?"

"Hang on, Stan. Let me put us in protection. Do you know that there is so much residual energy in this cottage, I'm having quite the job just separating individual spirits?"

Jim completed his prayer of protection, then explained the term "portal". "It basically means a gateway to and from another world, or realm. Vortex is another well-used term, meaning the same."

Sitting down to recover from the experience, Jim thought he needed more information about the house and land to determine its past history. Stan obliged by running up the stairs nervously and retrieving the local history book, along with the few papers Charlie had been reading. The gentle giant stared at Stan realising he was very scared. His big hand reached over to Stan's arm, gently holding it.

"Well, it's a good start, but look Stan, this place is not safe for you. Why don't you come over to my house, for the time being, at least."

Stan didn't argue about that. He felt far too uneasy anyway and gladly accepted the offer.

CHAPTER 8

Meanwhile, Charlie had her own problems. The man who pulled her into this strange world, seemed to be facing up to this darkened shadow, a shape that could only be described as half man, half beast. He held up a silver cross and chanted in Latin. The creature then disappeared without a trace.

"Hi, I'm Jack," he acknowledged, as he turned round to look at Charlie, who was completely disorientated and obviously very frightened.

"So you're Jack," Charlie cried out, "the one who went missing back in the forties? I'm supposed to be helping you, where the hell am I?"

"Sorry about that. My plan didn't quite work out as expected. I'll explain later, come on, we've got to get out of here. They'll be back!"

A deepened red glow loomed above their heads, some fifty or sixty feet high. The area that surrounded her seemed to be like a large cavern.

Jack helped her to her feet, then, almost flying, ran across the shingle layered floor with Charlie in tow. They headed towards an entrance, to make good their escape.

"Don't look back, miss, keep going!" Jack yelled at

Charlie, as tormented screams and loud shuffles advanced from behind them. They eventually came into the open air, still running, towards a spinney of trees. Fields surrounded the area, but there was something strange about this particular spinney though. It was upside down. The roots were actually sticking up into the air, with no sign of any leaves.

Upon entering into this mysterious, if not paradoxical, landscape, Jack declared that they were now safe from their pursuers.

Charlie was quite exhausted by this time, puffing and panting, urging the stranger to slow down. Moving deeper into the spinney, they came across a log cabin that had, to all sense and purpose, a moss-lined roof.

Here we are then," Jack pointed out. "Home at last."

Inside the hut stood a small table, a couple of chairs and an open log fire. It didn't matter to her where she was, all she wanted was to sit down and catch her breath. As soon as she finally regained her composure, as well as some dignity. Staring at this man Jack she realised that his clothing didn't match up to those of the seventies. She wondered if he was an actor, judging by his weird attire. Pushing her hair out of her eyes, arms resting on the man made table, angrily launched into Jack with a flurry of questions.

"Where the hell am I? What are those creatures? What is this hellish place?"

Moving across the dirt floor towards a small log fire, he raised his arm to stop the barrage of questions. "Whoa, hang on missy, I'll try to explain," he abruptly interrupted. Poking the almost distinguished fire, he tried to calm Charlie down. "For a start, you've come into a time dimension. In other words, you've gone back in time. Don't ask me how, I can't tell you. I just don't know. Those creatures, as you very delicately put them, are called Satanicals. They're devil beasts, straight from hell itself."

Jack sat, wiped his forehead, then continued. "These Satanicals have bodies that represent half man, half beast. They can easily kill a man with a single strike. The only defence against them, I have found, is shoving a silver cross into their faces. They believe, with good reason, that the cross is the symbol to be most feared. They avoid any contact with Him and his symbol."

Jack then went on to tell Charlie of the rituals that are practiced by the Satanicals.

"These creatures have created this time dimension, into which to draw unsuspecting human beings. They are put into some sort of trance. It could be a powerful drug they use, but in any case, they cast them into slaves. The slaves, or you might call them servants, are known as, Dronians. They perform satanic rituals against their own kind. It's not a pretty sight, I can tell you. So it's probably best if I don't tell you."

Charlie sat in complete disbelief and then asked where these Dronians lived.

"Before I go any further, what's your name?"

"You can call me Charlie." She repositioned herself on the harsh wooden chair.

"Well then, Charlie, since we have gone back into time, apart from the upside-down trees, everything in this area seems to be pretty normal, except that they are not. The people you might see are actually, Dronians. There's a village down yonder, just as it would have looked probably some time in the seventeenth century. But make no mistake, missy, they are not normal folk. I avoid them like the plague. If you didn't, you could soon become a victim of their rituals."

"And what about these trees? I wouldn't exactly call them normal."

"Ah yes, the locals call it the Ring of Roo, a God-given place of safety and holy sanctuary against all evil. Apparently..." Jack paused, got up and fetched a clay jug containing water. He placed two cups on the table offering Charlie a drink. "Satan tried to come to the surface of the earth, but the Lord God became angered, sent him back down into the bowels of the earth, then took the trees up with one hand and planted them, upside down, to ward off the evil creature."

"The trees are seen as God's creation and protection against Satan. And thank God he did, because I certainly wouldn't be here now and neither would you!"

"This is all very overwhelming," stuttered Charlie. "How come I was dragged into this world, when all I was trying to do was save you?"

"Yes, I'm sorry about that. It was just bad luck."

Charlie's patience finally floundered as she stared wildly at Jack. "Bad luck, bad luck, is that all you can say? You think that it was bad luck that you dragged me in, got me terrified of some sadistically creatures, told me of these so-called Dronians, who are people and yet aren't! This is just crazy. It's incredible. It can't be happening. This must be a damned nightmare!"

By now, Charlie was walking around the cabin, crying in utter disbelief.

"Calm down, missy." Beckoned Jack.

"And don't call me missy. My name is Charlie!"

"It seems you have a bit of a temper, Charlie?"

"No, I'm just upset, hungry, tired and frightened out of my wits! Stan will be having kittens by now, you've got to get me back."

Jack quickly changed the subject by telling her to rest for a little while he prepared something to eat. Charlie tended to calm down as she watched Jack go over to large iron pot and put it on the grid across the rejuvenated fire. He seemed very adept in his cooking methods, using freshly caught rabbits, duck, fish, birds and any amount of various eggs. There were signs of feathers, fur and odd scraps of eggshells. He told her that he also gathered wild corn, wheat and all manner of herbs. This day, however, would see him use up the last of the rabbit stew he had eaten the previous day.

After the meal, Charlie once again and in more detail, wanted to know why she happened to be dragged into this time dimension.

"Okay," replied Jack, "If you insist, but you'd better get comfortable first. " He eyed Charlie up and down, confusion settling over his face. "What on earth though, are those strange clothes you've got on? They'll never keep you warm."

She told him that they were pajamas, used for bedtime sleep, and if he hadn't shouted for help, she would already be tucked up, nice and cosy, with her husband.

He thought it strange that a woman would go to bed

wearing what looked like something a man would wear. He then passed her a large fur, which he obtained from a small room. He told her that he had made it from wolf hide.

"I reckon that'll keep you warmer than those silly things."

Charlie allowed him to wrap the heavy but warm hide, around her. Once again she sat on a chair, raised her legs up to the seat and completely emerged herself in the softness of the fur.

He explained by saying how he disguised himself as one of the Dronians. By hiding close to the cavern entrance, when the procession passed, he jumped onto the end. It gained him entrance to the cavern.

He told of the strange way the portal opened. Then, when the high priest or who he thought to be the high priest, came into the cavern, he would break off from the main procession and head towards one of the walls. The priest then chanted something in Latin, which caused the wall to shimmer. This shimmering then changed into a strange, greenish colour. The priest then made his way towards the altar where he joined the other chanting Dronians.

Large boulders were scattered to the left hand side of the cavern, close to the area where the portal opened. This area he thought, could be a good place to slip behind, away from the view of the guarding Satanicals and any Dronians. There seemed to be only two of these guards: one close to the main entrance and the other by the large stone altar.

Jack waited patiently. It was important the ceremony

begin first. This then, would be an ideal time to make good his escape.

"I didn't have to wait for very long," he murmured. "They brought in one of the villagers, a young female. She must have only been in her early twenties. She walked in silently, but seemingly of her own free will with one of the guards, who was guarding the entrance. She then stood by the altar while the Dronians stripped her naked." Charlie noticed how Jack must be feeling uncomfortable. He kept getting up from the table, rubbed his head then sat back down. Sighing, he continued.

"They then walked her to another slab of stone, this one had shackles attached to it."

"But why?" interrupted Charlie, "surely they would have put her on the slab first to sacrifice her?"

"I was just coming to that. The thing is, well, the Dronians were all men. I hate to say this, but, well, they all took off their robes. They were all naked underneath and then they all took it in turn to quite violently have sex with her."

"Oh my God." Charlie recoiled with one hand on her face. "Didn't she struggle, or

try to get free?"

"No, it was as if she didn't know what was happening. She was out of it. I suspect she had been given some sort of drug. At the altar, they gave her a drink. I don't know what it was, but I expect that it was a top-up, more drugs. Whatever it was, it must have been very powerful, because she was chanting away in Latin verses, along with the rest of the Dronians.

"After that, they released her from her shackles and

pushed her to the floor. The Satanical who had been by the altar then came across to her. It wasn't a pretty sight--what he did, but to cut the story short, he took her like a dog, on all fours. To say he was rough is an understatement. She didn't have much hair left on her head. Afterwards, I could see clearly she was bleeding badly, especially down her legs."

Charlie was horrified at Jack's words. Trickles of tears were now obvious upon her pretty face.

Jack looked at her, wondering whether this was all too much for her. "Maybe I should stop Charlie. This is distressing you too much."

Wiping the tears away with her hand she urged Jack on. After considering that if this sort of thing was to be stopped, then she needed to know the full story. Jack paused for a moment, sipping at his cup of water, then continued.

"Well, you're a plucky little thing, aren't you? Still, if that's the way you want it, then I'll carry on. After the Satanical had finished with her, she was stood up by the Dronians and marched off to the altar. This is where it gets a bit nasty, I'm afraid. The Dronians put their robes back on, then stood around the altar, after placing the girl there, lying on her back. Her hair, or should I say what was left of it, was covered in blood, as were her legs. It looked like she was bleeding quite badly from her private parts because the blood ran down the one end of the alter."

Again pausing for a while, perspiration showing on his face, Jack stood, then stared out the window, sighing slightly.

"Are you all right?" Charlie asked, but he just turned around and continued.

"Four of the Dronians held her down by her legs and arms, while the Satanical, who was at the head of the altar, passed a double bladed knife to the priest. He seemed to be chanting something or other, then, with the knife, cut up her stomach. I tell you, that poor girl was screaming in agony. It made no difference though, he just continued. I saw his hand plunge into her body and he pulled out what looked like her kidneys. He handed this blood-dripping organ to the Satanical who ate it with grisly laughter. I'm glad to say that the girl was already dead by now. As they continued their vile desecration, I took the opportunity to make my move while they were distracted. I thought that I was going to be sick, it took all my energy not to be.

"Since I was close to one of the large rocks I found it easy to move around. Those devils were too busy to notice me disappear, so I made for the portal, which was still open. It was very unfortunate for me, as well as yourself, because as I arrived at its entrance, you decided to make your appearance. When you put your hand in, it must have startled me and I just blurted out, 'help me'. The next thing I knew, a Satanical intervened and grabbed both our wrists, simultaneously. Where the hell he appeared from baffled me. The sheer speed of him took me completely by surprise.

"Fortunately, I managed to bring out the silver cross, which was tied around my neck. I thrust it into the evil creature's face. He didn't like that one bit, but at least I got him moving back. You, I'm afraid, were already sprawled out on the floor. The rest is history. Okay now? I think it's time to get some sleep. We've done enough talking for now. We'll continue tomorrow."

"Yes, you're right," Charlie yawned and stood up, "but where do I sleep?"

"Through that door over there. Don't worry, you'll be quite safe from me and anything else. I'm a little too old for any nonsense with women. If you do need anything just shout, my room is just opposite."

She looked a bit nervous, but she believed Jack to be a man of his word. Assured, she retired.

CHAPTER 9

Stan and Gentle Jim worked tirelessly in the library at Grantham. Books of the occult, ancient rituals and historical facts from the 17th century, along with myths and legends, were among the many they looked through. Many notes were made by both of them, which they would go through when they got back home.

Back at Jim's cottage, after first refreshing themselves with food and drink, the two men set about comparing their notes. A lot of information was found regarding the old village and its peculiar history, but little was found in terms of the graveyard, or the cottage that was built on top of it. They knew the graveyard had been re-interred in a village a few miles away.

"I think I might have it," Jim blurted out. "It has to do with the old graveyard, or, rather, the person or persons who were buried around the site of the cottage."

"What do you mean?" interrupted confused Stan. "Surely if they got all the remains out of the graveyard, then there shouldn't be any problems."

"Well, if that was indeed the case. But what if some of the bodies still remain? Now, if that's the case, who, exactly?"

Jim explained to Stan that he needed to look further back into the past when these satanic rituals were taking place.

"Some of these historical facts are not quite right. It says, according to most of the documentation, that the cottages were demolished. But this parish record states that the village was razed to the ground by fire. It says here that the Lord of the manor took charge of it personally."

They surmised that it was possible that some of the villagers could have perished in their own homes and their remains could have been subjected to very fast burials within the graveyard. If that was the way it was, then it was unlikely the church sanctified them.

"Just to sum it up, Stan, the evil still exists and that means, my friend, that your cottage is right at the centre of it all."

Pacing around the soft furnished room Stan's nervousness showed. "I'm sure you're right Jim, but how will all of this help get my Charlie back?"

"Well, Stan, normally I would send the spirits to the light. Heaven, if you like, where the angels would collect them. Then I would seal up the vortex. I can't do that, in this case, because we've got to get your wife out first and besides, these aren't exactly normal spirits. I need to know a bit more about these rituals, so what I'll do first is contact a friend of mine, who specializes in ancient black arts. If I understand the rituals, then, hopefully, it should help us gain entrance through the vortex."

CHAPTER 10

Charlie slept very well that night and awoke to the shimmer of sunlight, as it attempted to invade the mass of trees that surrounded the cabin. Everything looked quite normal to her, as she lay there thinking Jack really was a gentleman, keeping to his word. The log cabin seemed to have a particular aura to it, so natural in design, so rustic, warm and surprisingly very comfortable. Listening intensely, she could hear the birds, singing their wonderful morning chorus. The unmistakable sound of something sizzling in a pan made her feel very hungry. Just at that moment, Jack shouted, "breakfast is ready."

She tried to rouse herself from the comfortable bed but felt so secure and cosy under the eiderdown quilt, it became a struggle. The gorgeous smell though soon got the better of her. Wandering into the main room she saw that a very ornate wooden table was laden with one plate containing two eggs and a freshly cooked loaf of bread.

"Not quite the Savoy, I'm afraid," Jack announced putting the pan down as he came and sat at the table, "but at least it's food."

With a sharp knife, he sliced the bread into thick pieces, then handed her a slice.

Accepting the bread, smiling at the cook, she thanked him with eagerness. No hesitation adorned her mind, as she quickly demolished this heaven-sent meal.

"Hmm, that was wonderful. Jack, I didn't know you kept chickens."

"Those weren't no chicken eggs." He laughed. "They were duck eggs, fresh this morning."

Charlie looked surprised. "You mean you've been out already?"

"Of course I have, best time to catch the ducks napping! Don't worry about it, you'll soon learn."

Charlie wondered why he said this. After all, the only thing on her mind was to get back to the normal world. Pondering on this, she asked Jack when they would be able to make their escape.

"About two weeks," he announced, "with any luck, provided they keep to their yearly schedule."

"What do you mean, yearly schedule, Jack?"

"Well, basically, this ritual they hold is only performed one week before summer solstice, then again two weeks later. If we miss this next opportunity, then I'm afraid we'll have to wait until next year."

"Next year? I've just gotten married!"

"That's unfortunate, but if we are to get out of here, then we have a lot of work to do."

Getting up from the table, Charlie walked to the door and opened it, taking in a breath of fresh air. Her mind drifted to her husband, Stan. How was he coping? Would he be trying to get her out? There were many things going on in Charlie's mind that confused her. In reality, though, she knew he would try his best to do something.

"I imagine, you know, Jack, that my husband, Stan, will be trying to get us out of here. He's very resourceful you know."

"Well, I hope he is. We could do with all the help we can get." Jack agreed, putting the wooden plates they had just eaten from into a pail of water. Charlie started asking more questions.

"How long have you been here Jack? Why is there another bedroom?"

"Why, why, why, geez woman, are you always like this? You'll give me a headache.

"I'm sorry Jack, it's just that I'm anxious. Can I help you with anything?"

Tell you what, sit down, I'll make a brew, then I'll tell you all my history."

Charlie watched with interest as Jack set a pan of water on the fire, added herbs, then some stinging nettles. These were freshly picked when Jack had gone out in the early hours of the morning.

"Ah, nettle tea," he said as he stirred furiously, "do you a world of good."

Charlie stayed silent, watching with great interest, although thinking she would rather have a proper cup of tea. As it turned out, the brew tasted quite nice, a bit pungent, maybe, too many bits floating around the cup, but still, not bad.

"If you need it sweeter, there's a jar of honey on the shelf, I only got it two days ago, mind you, can't say the bee's were very happy though." Charlie declined the offer and burst out laughing, as did Jack. He told her that he used it for some of his meals or just to give him some extra energy.

"What year is it?" he asked finally sitting down.

Charlie thought it curious that he didn't know. "It's 1975."

"Hmm, looks like I've lost a few years. Never mind. Now then, let's see."

Jack paused a little as he tried to remember the date he got stranded in this strange underworld.

"Ah yes, it would have been 1910 when I moved into the cottage. In fact, it was not long after old Thomas Beaumont had disappeared. I'll tell you more about him later. The Second World War came and I can remember Carberry Manor being blown up by the Luftwaffe. I wonder whatever happened to the old place. You might be able to tell me about that later."

Charlie frowned. "I don't need to wait until later, you know, Jack, because I've never heard of the place."

Jack sipped at his drink, "That does surprise me. Carberry Manor is your ancestral home. I thought you would have at least heard of it. So where were you raised then?" Grinning, he raised his fingers together.

"Whitehaven Hall, in Oxford," she quipped.

"Hmm, well, there must be a good reason for George to keep it from you," the indignant Jack retorted. Failing to question Charlie any further, Jack pressed on. He told her how, that at the same time the manor got bombed, he too was having strange things happen in the cottage. It resembled the same type of events that had entangled Charlie. He, too, had gotten caught up in the portal, but somehow managed to miraculously escape from the demons. Once outside, a man named Thomas, who took him to the cabin he now lived in, soon found him.

"Very strange that was really. I found out he was a long lost friend and indeed a cousin of the Carberry family.

"Hang on a minute," interrupted Charlie. "If he was a close cousin, what is your surname?"

"I thought you might have guessed that I'm a Carberry."

"Good God, then we're related! I'm a Carberry, Charlotte Carberry. My father is George Alfred Carberry."

"Well then, there's a surprise," gulped Jack. "George is my younger brother, by about twelve years. That, my dear niece, makes me your uncle!"

Silence dawned for a while, as they stared at each other, not quite knowing what to do or say. Both smiling, Charlie laughed as she stood to shake hands with her newfound uncle.

"Well, uncle, it's a pleasure to meet you, but why didn't I know about your existence?"

"Can't answer that one, I'm afraid. You'll have to ask your father. Perhaps it's because of the family curse!"

"What do you mean, family curse? Nothing like this has ever been mentioned to me."

"I don't suppose it has, Charlie. George wouldn't have any of this sort of rubbish. He would probably just dismiss it, then order the household to never mention it. They say that this curse originated many years ago in this very place we are in now. From what I have learned, this place was called Maplewood, a village of great evil that included devil worship. As you probably know, witchcraft was very much frowned upon, especially by the church

58

who made quite a meal of it. Condemned witches would have been stoned to death, burned at the stake or ducked into a river until they drowned. Maplewood was no exception.

"It was found that when Lord Alfred Carberry knew of the witchcraft, he ordered the old village to be burnt down and the ringleader, along with his cronies, burnt at the stake. It was this ringleader who cursed the family name by saying, 'thou shalt see'eth thy inheritance in Satan's land. I await thee and curse thy name from here on'. Looks like his curse is still ongoing, since here we are."

Charlie frowned, yet found the story very intriguing. Her imagination was now running wild.

"But what happened to Thomas?" she asked.

"Thomas, oh yes, the old fool," grunted Jack, "too slow and too old. Unfortunately, he couldn't get out of the way of the villagers when trying to steal some knives and oddments. They caught him when he wasn't wearing his silver cross, which gives us some protection. He's dead now, the Dronians ripped him to shreds. It was horrible. There was nothing I could do for him. Oh I tried, Jesus I tried hard, but there were too many of them. I barely got out myself, it was only because I was wearing my cross that saved me."

"Oh my God," Charlie said with a very frightened expression. "And you've escaped capture all these years?"

"It hasn't been easy, but I've survived. You will too, providing you listen and only do what I say."

Charlie agreed that she would. "Have you a plan?" she asked.

"Yes," he replied, "but it will be dangerous. My idea is to collect whatever silver we can find then melt it down to form crosses. These crosses will give us protection around the portal in the cavern. If we can manage to create a half circle with them in front of the portal, then we can pass through to the world that we came from. Make no mistake though, Charlie. While this all sounds simple, it won't be easy at all. They'll be on their guard, especially now that they know you are here. They much prefer women for their sacrifices."

"But why only a half circle of crosses," Charlie inquisitively asked.

"Okay, imagine a full circle with a line drawn horizontally across its centre. Put the portal wall on that line and that's what we see on our side, just half of a circle. Once this is done and we are inside our half, the Satanicals or the Dronians cannot enter."

"Yes, that sounds fine, but can the Dronians remove them?"

"Aye, possibly, but I don't that they would commit themselves in too much of a hurry. Saying that, if it was a complete circle, then there wouldn't be any problem at all. It's a pity someone on the other side couldn't form the other half, then even the Dronians couldn't go near them. Maybe your husband can come up trumps."

"Stan is probably working on it right now, knowing him," Charlie confessed.

"Well if he does," said Jack cautiously, "it would help us to seal up this monstrous world for good!"

"There's something else I'd like to ask you Jack, if you don't mind?"

"Go ahead girl, I'll get no rest until you do."

"Sorry Jack, it's my inquisitive nature. So tell me, why did you live in the cottage, rather than the manor?"

"What a strange thing to ask. Still, it's quite simple really. Well my dear niece, my father wasn't the easiest person to get along with. We tended to clash a little, but I decided I needed a little bit of space and independence. A bit like you, if I'm not mistaken. Anyway I just asked him for the little cottage and it was given to me. We didn't argue as such, more a sense of understanding each other. I did love him, very much, but the thought of a little quietness would inspire my work. I'm a writer you see, needed my own space. Don't get me wrong, the manor was fine, very popular in fact. I suppose that was the trouble, it was too popular. There were too many parties, people coming and going, everyone wanting to know what one was doing. I just couldn't stand it and that is all there is to it, okay now?"

"Yes, thanks Jack," she laughed. "It's nice to know that I'm not the only odd one in the family!"

CHAPTER 11

Detective Inspector Russell Brown was handed the case files and chosen as the most appropriate person to lead the investigation into the disappearance of Charlie. Being of high rank and well thought of by his superiors and colleagues, he dealt with unusual cases like this, as he made them his speciality.

Over a week had passed since Charlie's disappearance and the normal avenues of Russell Brown's investigation hadn't bought forward any positive leads whatsoever. A knock on his office door saw the bulky frame of the sergeant.

"This is very strange, you know, Sergeant Wilder. I mean, who could possibly come up with a wild story about disappearing into a wall? It doesn't make sense, Sergeant, no indeed, no sense at all!"

Sergeant Wilder, standing six foot three, his large frame earning him the nickname "Bulldozer Wilder," towered over the Inspector's desk. Not looking up from his papers, the wiry inspector made up for it with his unique sense of humour and brilliance. He dressed like the famous Columbo, raincoat and all. Despite his looks, the eccentric gent gave the impression of a great philosopher. His record in solving crimes was one of the best in the county.

The sergeant, smiling, agreed with him, then handed the inspector the report on Stan's past.

"I think you'll find this intriguing sir. It appears that this man has a habit for losing his women."

"Really?" replied the inspector, looking up at the sergeant with some surprise. The sergeant then walked out, closing the door quietly. With a careful eye on detail, the detective fingered slowly through the files, pausing only to re-read a paragraph that he had already read. It was about an hour later that the inspector came out of his office and ordered the sergeant to get any new updates from Interpol concerning one Stanley Harrow.

"I'm going over to Little Leaf, if anybody needs me," he told the sergeant as he quietly and, without any rush of urgency, took his khaki-colored raincoat from the coat stand, thinking to himself as he did so that this particular item had seen better times.

Meanwhile, Stan had moved back into his cottage, along with Gentle Jim, who, by his mere presence, was the only one who could protect Stan from any invasion of these demons. A knock on the door disturbed their talking and they paused, wondering who it could possibly be at this time of night. Strolling over to the door, Stan was confronted by this stranger in an old raincoat.

"Mr Stanley Harrow, I presume? I'm Detective Inspector Brown. I wonder if I may take a little of your time?" The detective had his warrant card at the ready, showing it to Stan.

"Please do come in, Inspector. Is there any news?" Stan asked.

"Why would there be any news, Sir, considering that you've told us that your wife disappeared through a wall! I don't very often have to deal with this sort of thing, Sir, so you'll excuse me if I don't quite understand. Perhaps you could just run me through the events of the night in question?"

Upon entering, the detective spotted Jim, sitting at the table. Looking him up and down, he coyly glared at him.

"Ah, good evening, Sir. It seems I know your face from somewhere?"

"Yes, that's correct, Inspector. I'm Jim Hawkins. You may remember me from when I gave a talk on the world of the medium. I think that it was last October, for one of the charity events that you run."

Putting his hand to his chin and looking a little puzzled, the inspector finally remembered the night of Jim's lecture.

"Ah yes, that was very interesting, Sir. Thank you for that. We must do it again sometime. It was very interesting. But tell me, Sir, why are you here? Do you have some sort of involvement with Mr Harrow?"

Gentle Jim explained to the inspector how he became involved with Stan. He listened very intensely and with great interest then turned to face Stan.

"I wonder if perhaps you could just go over your story for me now Sir, just to clear up any misunderstandings and to clarify the facts."

The detective was offered a seat at the table then Stan, although frustrated at having to repeat his story, eagerly recalled the events of that horrifying night.

"Hmm," the inspector paused, "this mysterious wall, Sir, perhaps you could show it to me."

The three men strolled into the lounge where Inspector Brown examined the wall. "It looks quite normal to me, if you don't mind me saying, Sir. There aren't any secret passageways are there, Sir?"

"No, Inspector, not to my knowledge anyway." Stan repeated as he brushed back his dark hair.

"I didn't think so, but I have to ask. You'd be surprised at what some people hide you know. Anyway, it's just a wall, isn't it, Sir? Your wife, you say she somehow passed through it?"

Beleaguered, Stan could only agree with the common sense the inspector spoke. He was being humiliated by this line of questioning and felt some anger and desperation, knowing that he was not being believed.

"It doesn't surprise me that you don't believe me, Inspector, but I am telling you the truth. Believe me, I find it just as incredible as you do, but I think an open mind should be exercised here. After all, not all things on this earth are explainable. At least I am seeking answers, that's why I have a professional medium, who does, and more to the point, can, provide some answers!"

The inspector once again rubbed at his chin. "I'll tell you a secret, Sir, it's not that I don't believe in the supernatural, I've always said that there's more to life than meets the eye. Heaven knows, Sir, my own wife is always disappearing, but I can usually work it out where she is. But I've got a bit of a dilemma you see, Sir, I can't really go around putting in reports about the supernatural. My chief would think I've lost the plot. You can understand that, can't you, Sir?"

Pausing for a moment, in the quietness of the room, the inspector continued his deliberation.

"Tell you what, Sir, perhaps you could come down to the station tomorrow and make a statement. That should keep my chief off my back, what do you think, Sir?"

"Yes, I'll do that inspector."

"Maybe you could also do the same for me, Mr, what did you say your name was, Sir?"

"Oh, Jim Hawkins." replied Jim smiling coyly at the detective.

"Of course, of course, Mr Hawkins!" he replied waving his hands in the air. With that, the inspector bid farewell and returned to the station.

Jim turned to Stan in astonishment. "I don't like the look of this Stan. I've seen his sort before. Believe me, that inspector won't let loose of a case like this. It's just too bizarre for them to understand."

"Yes, you're probably right," considered Stan, "but what can we do?"

"Well," Jim thought out loud. "If, for some reason, they decide to keep you in for questioning, then you'll just have to rely on me. The best thing to do is to give me a set of keys for the cottage. At least I'll be able to continue my work here."

Stan didn't seem to be in a position to argue, so he gave him the set of spare keys.

"I don't think it will come to that," said Stan, "well, I hope not anyway, but I suppose it's wise to take precautions."

The telephone startled Stan as it suddenly blurted out an irritating ring. He picked it up only to find that it was Charlie's father.

"Hello Stanley. George here, where have you been all week? I've been trying to telephone you. Nothing wrong, is there, old chap?"

Stan was taken aback, not knowing quite how to answer his question.

"Yes, sorry George, I'm afraid there is a bit of a problem. Charlie has gone missing!"

Stan tried hard to explain what had happened, but it took him some time.

"My good Lord," cried George. "Mildred will be very upset, very upset indeed! I'll be down tomorrow!"

Stan still held the telephone in his hand, even when George had put his down. He mumbled, "that's all I need tomorrow!"

"So, we'll have company tomorrow, will we?" Jim asked.

"Yes, but I should have told him earlier. Now he'll wonder why? I don't have any excuse for not phoning him. I'm just a bit bewildered by all of this! I hope he understands."

It seemed to Stan that the whole world had caved in on him.

Jim gave him all the reassurance he could, but reality had sunk in. It seemed as if the ghost's of the past had not finished with him yet. 'Will I ever be free of these hauntings?' Stan wondered in his mind. He was brought back to reality with Jim's change of subject.

"Oh, by the way Stan, I'm meeting my friend tomorrow afternoon. You remember, the one I told you about: Theodore, the expert on demonic rituals."

Stan nodded fetching another bottle of wine, pouring

some into two glasses. He handed one to Jim, spilling it slightly with his nervous hand.

"Yes, I remember. Let's hope we can learn something from him."

CHAPTER 12

Charlie stood quietly outside the door of the cabin, pondering the mysterious arrangement of the massive root structures above her head. She wondered what sort of power could possibly invert trees like this? Did God, really intervene? Just the thought of this immense power sent a shiver running down her spine. She clutched the four-inch silver cross that hung around her neck. Jack had given it to her earlier. He told her never to take the cross off for any reason whatsoever. Mortal danger would ensue if she did. She thanked the Lord for his protection, albeit in a whispered prayer.

At that point, Jack appeared at her side, startling her.

"Oh my gosh, Jack. You frightened the life out of me. I never even heard you come out!"

"No and if I can do that, then so can the Dronians. You must always be on your guard, keep alert and above all else, tread like a snake, slithering across the ground. One more thing, Charlie. Never go out of the boundary of the woods on your own!"

"You've got no worry about that! She exclaimed raising her eyebrows. "Why are you holding that bow and those arrows? Are you going hunting?"

"No I'm not, but you, my dear Charlie, are going to learn how to use them." Jack thrust them into Charlie's arms.

Jack took her a few yards from the cabin and pointed to an outward stretched limb of a tree.

"Watch how I do this," he exclaimed as he took his own bow from his shoulder. With the arrow settling on his tightly clenched bow, he drew back the hand-made string, two fingers lightly keeping the feathers of the arrow close to his chin. Aiming slightly above his target, the arrow was sent off in a devastating burst of speed. It hit its target so hard, that it split it along its entire length.

"Wow," gasped Charlie, "who taught you, Robin Hood?" She smiled, as she looked him up and down. His attire consisted of a warm fur jacket over a distinguished green tunic. Leather pants were made from some poor animal that served him well, while hand made soft moccasins were neatly stitched together. He only appeared to be about five feet four in height, but although he was small, his stance was tall and proud.

"Not quite my girl. I don't suppose you've ever done this sort of thing, have you?"

"No, I haven't, but it looks fun. Do I need to learn now then? If you can shoot as well as you do, why bother?"

"Two things Charlie: what if I got captured or killed. How would you feed and protect yourself?"

She went a little white with this thought. "Okay, I get the point, but don't expect me to be anywhere near as good as you!" she retorted.

Jack didn't really expect too much from a mere

woman, or so he thought, so it came as a bit of a shock to him when she took possession of the bow, raised it up, aimed and fired away her shot. It hit the tree with an almighty thump, which pleased her because she didn't think she could do it. Turning to Jack with a slight grin on her face, she asked him if her shot was all right.

"Magnificent!" said the stunned man. "Are you sure you've never taken archery lessons?"

Charlie told him that she hadn't. It seemed as if she was a natural archer. She, once again, tightened her grip on the bow and repeated the event with another arrow, which was very close to the first.

Jack made it much harder for her after that, by placing smaller obstacles in various positions and at varying heights. Charlie wasn't quite as good with these smaller obstacles, but, with practice, she improved. His gentle sense of persuasion and experience encouraged her as she learned all that Jack wanted to teach her.

A smile broadened upon her face as Jack told her that she was doing very well.

"Right then," Jack said, "I'm going to leave you to practice. I've got work to do and, for heaven's sake, don't point the bow in my direction. I'm only going to be by the cabin."

Charlie continued to practice with the bow, seemingly getting better with every shot she made. After about two hours of non-stop practice, her arms were just about to give up. With aches and pains, she headed back to the cabin only to find Jack stoking up some sort of furnace.

Inquisitively, she wandered over to Jack and asked him what he was doing.

"I'm melting down odd bits of silver. After that, I will use it to make more arrow heads!"

"Why silver?" asked Charlie. "Surely the arrows we have will pierce any animal or human being?"

"Yes, that might well be the case. The problem is, who said any of these humanoid beings are like us? While they may look human, they certainly don't die like us. No my girl, only silver-tipped arrowheads will actually destroy these monsters. You mustn't be fooled by their normal appearance or manner. Once they are on to you, they'll rip you to shreds without any questions!"

The heat from the furnace made Charlie step back a little, as Jack pumped the bellows at the bottom of the hot embers. The furnace was built with hard stone that Jack had retrieved from a small river, not far from the cabin. A hard mortar cemented the stones to form a round structure that had a small opening at the top. A pair of metal tongs gripped a heavy metal basin that contained the molten silver.

"Stand back a little, Charlie," warned Jack. "This is extremely hot."

She moved cautiously as Jack poured the molten substance into what looked like a wooden box.

"Won't that burn the box?" she exclaimed.

"No, it's just a case. Inside is clay, the case keeps the mold together. The silver, when I pour it into the hole at the top, will run into the chambers. In about half an hour, I'll open the box, turn out the baked clay and then break it open. You'll see!"

Putting down the now empty basin, Jack removed the bellows and turned to look at Charlie. He saw that she had bruising on her arm, her face red and perspiring.

"Been in the wars, have we? How did you get that bruise on your arm?"

"Oh, its nothing," she giggled, "the bow and I had an argument, the bow won!"

"Don't tell me, you let go of the bow instead of the string."

"Yes, something like that. It's a bit sore though."

Jack took her to the cabin, telling her that he had some ointment that would help the bruising and any pain. He produced a bottle of lotion with a sweet, smelling odour. He gently rubbed some into Charlie's arm.

"What is it?" she asked, squirming with Jack's attention. She noticed a sweet aroma scent the air around her.

"It's witch hazel mainly," he replied, "but with a touch of a pain relief ingredient."

Taking in the wonderful aroma, she felt a small tingling sensation where Jack had rubbed the liniment into her arm.

"Hmm, that's lovely. How did you make it then, Jack? I couldn't see you buying it at the local chemist."

Jack laughed. "They don't have places like that around here, more's the pity. No my girl. I use natural herbs, like the foxglove! Good for the heart, arthritis and as a pain relief. There are many herbs you could use for different ailments. Look over here." He showed Charlie different bottles of herbs and mixtures, "How about this one," he pointed out, "It's called Yarrow. It helps you stop bleeding, if you get cut. Stinging nettles on the other hand, well, you've already had some of that. It was your drink, makes good beer as well. There's a lot to learn if you want to survive Charlie, but for the moment, let's go and look at our new arrowheads."

Charlie was amazed at the knowledge Jack had gained. She also felt pleased and comforted to know she was in very good and capable hands. After a little while, they walked back outside to the furnace area where Jack had left the now cooled down molds. He opened the box and knocked out the heavy clay mold. Picking up a small metal hammer, he cracked it open with very little force. The arrowheads that protruded from the lumps of broken clay were all but perfectly formed. After a little cleaning in water, they were shining as brightly as the sunshine.

CHAPTER 13

Stan awoke the next morning, hurriedly got dressed and went downstairs to open the front door. He took in the sound of birds singing their beautiful songs. The sun, shining its golden rays across fields of barley and corn, made for stunning scenery. He took in several deep breaths of the clean, fresh air.

"Good morning, Stanley. Sleep well?" echoed the booming voice of Jim.

Turning to see Jim doing up his shirt buttons, Stan was taken aback to see him already up and about.

"Ah, morning, Jim. It's a fine day, don't you think?"

"Certainly is. Are you ready for the day's trials? It's not going to be easy for you."

"I think so, but I could do without it."

Well, I hope so. Best get some breakfast and get down to the station. We'll take both cars though. I'll need to be going straight over to the train station, to pick up my friend, I'll bring him straight back here, just in case your wife's father turns up."

"Okay Jim, oh, and by the way Jim, thanks for all you're doing. I don't know what I'd do without you."

It didn't take long for the two men to make and eat

their breakfast. Soon after, they were on their way to the police station.

Greeted by Sergeant Wilder, Jim was taken to an interview room. A second police officer took Stan to a different one. Detective Brown arrived on the scene and asked Stan if he would like a cup of tea, but he politely declined. The room appeared quite small having only a single window, three hard chairs that were around a small table and a shelf with a tape recorder perched on it's top.

"Be with you in one minute, Sir. I have to put a tape in this machine you see. Saves a lot of time so there's no mistakes made."

Just then, another police officer walked in, carrying a large file.

"Ah yes, this is Constable Munrose. He'll be sitting in with us to take the statement. Now then, Sir, let's just start from the beginning, shall we? You tell me the events leading up to the time that your wife vanished."

The detective sat in silence as Stan, once again, told his story.

"After I got home from work and had something to eat, my wife and I were sitting talking. We noticed a strange light illuminating from the wall. Charlie, my wife, decided to investigate it, with me by her side. We heard a faint voice coming from some sort of doorway. I now know that this phenomenon is called either a 'portal' or a ''vortex'. I was very concerned about her going too close, but she insisted. I took hold of her hand while she reached out into this 'portal'. The next thing I knew, she was suddenly pulled from my grasp into the portal and vanished. It caught me by surprise and as I went to try and do the same, I got an awful type of electric shock, which threw me to the floor. Of course I tried to get in once again, but found that the portal had disappeared. There was nothing I could do." Stan waved his hand in exasperation. "I then came to see you here, at the police station. After that, I managed to find Mr Hawkins. He's been helping me try to resolve the situation."

"Yes, indeed. Tell me, Mr Harrow, do you have a problem with misplacing or losing many of your women?"

"What do you mean?" he angrily inquired, "I don't make a habit of losing women at all!"

Picking up a piece of paper from the file, the detective quickly gazed back at Stan. "Well sir, I'm afraid that you do precisely that. What about your previous girlfriend, in Australia if I'm correct?"

Stan was taken by surprise. The sudden realization of his past life was now to be raked up, once again.

"I must protest, Inspector. That has nothing to do with what's happened recently!"

"I'm afraid it does, Sir. You see, that the Australian authorities never closed this particular case. It couldn't, you see, because there wasn't any body or remains found. Just like now, if you get my drift."

"Look, Inspector, I've told you the truth, just as I did in Australia, with the authorities there. They even said it was probably a drowning or that the crocodiles took her. Why don't you believe me?"

"Tell you what, Mr Harrow. Why don't you ask anyone in this station if they would believe your story? It's a bit wild really by anyone's standards. Now you can see my predicament. I suggest you had an awful argument, things probably got a little out of hand, you hit out at her, just a little bit too hard, the blow killed her and you disposed of the body. It happens from time to time. You probably panicked. I can understand that Sir, especially if she had a bit of a temper! Is that the way it was, Sir?"

"No, no, I never lifted a hand to my wife, ever. I love her and that's the truth! Inspector, I've only just got married, do you honestly think that I'm some sort of sadistical monster?"

Detective Inspector Russell Brown stood, walked to the tape machine then turned to look at Stan with a questioning expression.

"Interview suspended, time, eleven a.m. A word with you, Constable, if you please."

Turning the machine off and leaving the room, the two police officers stood, whispering to each other.

"Your opinion, Constable?"

"He's taking us for fools, Sir! One missing person, maybe, but two? His story is just too far fetched, and that's if you believe in the supernatural at all. No sir, I neither believe him nor trust him."

"Thank you, Constable. What did you say your name was again?"

"Munrose, Sir. David Munrose."

"Well David, I want you to set up a forensic search of the house, do it now for me, would you? I'll obtain the warrant, then meet you and the team at the house."

Before departing on their way, the detective and constable went back into the interview room. Stan was pacing the floor as they re-entered.

"I'm afraid that we will have to hold onto you for a while, Mr Harrow. There are a few more details for me to go over, you see? Oh, and by the way, you won't mind if we do a little search of your house, will you?"

"I protest. You can't hold me without a charge, surely?" Stan defiantly said.

"Yes, Sir, I can, for twenty four hours. Don't worry, Sir. I'll try my best not to delay you any longer than I need."

"Inspector, before you go you should know that Jim Hawkins will probably be at the cottage. He has my permission to be there."

"Thank you, Sir. I'll bear that in mind. One last thing, Sir, I will require your keys."

Stan knew it was best to co-operate and handed the detective a few keys that hung from a lucky charm key ring. Not quite so lucky, he thought.

He was then taken to a cell, which was located in the basement of the police station. His belongings were taken from him, along with his shoelaces. The steel door, with its shuttered peephole centered at head height, slammed shut, as the turn of a key confirmed that he was truly locked into this small, solitary space.

The unforgiving solitude of the cell held only a single bed and a small urinal. Sitting on the edge of the bed, hands clasping his face, he looked down at his lace-less shoes. He tried to digest the meaning of this paradox. 'Did they really think I might take my own life? How would one use such small insignificant items like shoe laces anyway?' These thoughts contradicted everything he believed in and understood. Even the miserly contents of his pockets now infiltrated the corners of a small plastic bag, hidden away in a dark box of metal.

"This is ridiculous!" he muttered to himself, but the thought of his wife being in some sort of hellish hole, terrified and frightened out of her mind, brought him back to reality.

Arriving at the cottage, warrant in hand, the intrigued inspector knocked on the door, not really expecting anyone to answer. He stood slightly back as the door was indeed answered. A tall, thick-set gentle giant, Jim Hawkins, filled the entire doorway.

"Ah, Mr Hawkins, I was told that you may be here. I have a search warrant here, I wonder if you wouldn't mind stepping aside to allow my team to enter?"

The quiet, undeterred detective gave the warrant to Jim Hawkins, who immediately moved aside. Two men in white overalls entered the premises, followed by two constables. One of them, Constable Munrose, disappeared up the stairs.

The two men, dressed in white overalls, made their way to the front lounge. It seemed the wall that bore the portal, along with the surrounding floor and furniture, was the main area of interest.

Inspector Russell Brown seemed more preoccupied by the presence of someone he had not seen before. Gazing at this tall, thin structure of a person of African-origin, it was obvious to the detective that he should know more about this stranger.

"I don't believe I have the pleasure of knowing who you are, Sir?"

Jim Hawkins immediately spoke out, at that point.

"My apologies, Inspector. This is Theodore Philips, a friend of mine. Mr Harrow is aware that he will be here. He will be aiding my investigation."

"I'm intrigued, Mr Philips. Perhaps we could all sit at the table and have a little chat." The questioning detective inquired.

"Let me first explain the presence of Theodore," gentle Jim infused. "Mr Philips is a well renowned author and expert on ritual ceremonies of the black arts. I believe that with his specialist knowledge of these matters, we will be able to uncover the mysterious goings-on within these walls and find the solution to getting back Stan's wife, Charlotte."

"Well, Sir, Mr Philips, oh, and by the way Mr Philips, it is an honour, indeed a pleasure, for me to be in such distinguished company. Mr Harrow should be very fortunate to have such distinguished persons acting on his behalf! But tell me, gentlemen, why does what Mr Harrow has told you make you more inspired to believe in his story?"

"May I, as an outsider to this area and its occupants, be allowed to explain our reasons?" interrupted Theodore with a serious face, his dark eyes piercing through the very fabric of the inspectors face.

"Yes, please do indeed, Mr Philips. That would be a good idea," said the Inspector, who, by now seemed bemused by this stranger.

"Let me first say that we need to look at the bigger picture." Began Theodore. "What I mean is that not only do we look at this one particular occurrence, in this case this very cottage and what has happened, but we also need to look at what historical interventions of the local area have also occurred within the past."

"Hold up one moment, Sir. Are you trying to tell me that this sort of thing has happened in the past?"

"Yes, Mr Brown, sorry, Inspector. That is exactly what we are saying. This place, in fact the whole village, has a history you may find hard to believe or digest, because of it being kept a well guarded secret. We are, in fact, talking about satanic rituals taking place. There were people being tortured. The village was burnt to the ground and some of the inhabitants were burnt at the stake. Even the graveyard vanished, or it got moved to another site."

"Well, good Lord," the inspector looks around the cottage wiping his brows with a handkerchief, "this is all, so very interesting, but how does all of this have any bearing on the disappearance of a woman within these past few weeks?"

"Quite simple, Inspector, unfinished business!"

"Forgive me Mr Philips, sir, what exactly do you mean, unfinished business?"

"If you'll allow me," interrupted Jim, "I'll take over from here. You see, Inspector, when the village was burnt to the ground, the main ringleaders were burnt at the stake. While this was in progress, the leader put a curse on the Carberry family. The Carberrys owned the village and it was Lord Carberry who ordered the destruction of the village and the execution of the members of the satanic cult. I have uncovered a document that gives proof of a curse. I have the document here, in fact. Would you like to hear the contents of this curse?"

"Indeed I would, Sir!"

"Very well. It reads, 'thou shalt see'eth thy inheritance in Satan's land, I await thee Carberry. Cursed be thy name from this day forward'. So, Inspector, we now have a curse which, I might add, was taken very seriously by the folk of those times. In fact, we have recorded evidence that shows of mysterious occurrences taking place at this cottage. This includes the disappearance of some people, which included members of the Carberry family. In fact, Inspector, and you can probably look this up in your records, one particular man, Jack Beaumont, disappeared suddenly in 1942. No evidence was ever found as to what actually happened to him. He simply disappeared without a trace. Now, this man is the person we think called out for help when the portal opened. According to Stan Harrow, his wife was convinced that it was Jack that called out to her. This caused her to take the action she did."

The inspector gazed at Jim while slowly stroking his chin. Contemplating this behaviour, Jim knew the inspector wanted to say something.

"Mr Hawkins, Sir, it seems that you have been doing your homework. Your interpretation of events is very interesting. Let's say what you're telling me is the truth. It still does not explain why this 'portal', or whatever it may be, happens to be in this particular cottage. Why is it not happening at Carberry Manor, since this is the main dwelling of this family?"

"I'm just coming to that Inspector. We believe that this has to do with the missing graveyard. The way that we see it is that not all of the graves were actually removed. In particular, we are not certain what happened to the remains of the Satanists who died at the stake, all those many years ago."

"This is where I come in," interrupted the dark figure of Theodore. "I have studied many aspects of different cultures that worship Satan. There are many varying styles of rituals that these cults adhere to. For instance, one certain tribe in western Africa would sacrifice humans of a certain age then dismember their bodies. They would keep the head and boil it clean to the skull, which was then put on display, in a cave. The rest of the body would be fed to the piranhas that swam in the river. They believed that the piranhas were sent from Satan himself and therefore, needed to appease him."

"Hold on there, Sir," the soft-voiced inspector insisted, "I don't quite understand what this has to do with missing remains and this cottage?"

"Sorry, Inspector, it is a little confusing, isn't it? Simply then, if the remains are close to this cottage, then it would explain why a portal exists within it. You see, the spirits of the remains would be attracted to this area and so they make an entrance, a portal, from their world to ours. They can come and go, at will."

The inspector rose from his chair as one of the forensic people came towards him. Whispering took place between the pair of them, and then the forensic team took their leave. They were soon followed by the two constables. The bemused inspector then turned to speak to Stan and Theodore.

"Well, gentlemen, it has been an experience for me to listen to such devoted people. I have learned much. But now I must return to the station. Thank you for indulging your thoughts with me."

CHAPTER 14

Half an hour had passed since the inspector departed from the cottage when a series of rapturous knocks on the door of the cottage. It made Jim jump a little. Removing his large frame from the chair, he strolled over to the door, only to find Charley's father, George, standing there like a sergeant major.

"What the blue blazes is going on here and who might you be, Sir?" said the thundering voice of George Carberry.

"I'm Jim Hawkins and you must be Charlie's father, please do come in!"

"Jim Hawkins, eh, what? Ah, aren't you that spiritualist chap?"

"Yes, Sir, I am. I'm afraid your son-in-law has been detained for questioning at the police station."

George looked around the room, then noticed Theodore coming in from the kitchen.

"My God, there's another one." Blazed George.

"Let me introduce Mr Theodore Philips. He's helping me in my work." Jim tried to explain.

"Your work, Sir?" What exactly is your work? I think you had better start telling me what has gone on here!"

Jim offered him a drink of Scotch, then they sat down and Jim told him the whole story. Jim was a little surprised when, after he was finished telling George what had happened, the aging MP simply announced he had "rather expected something like this to happen", although he hoped it had by now been finished with.

"Do you know of the curse, sir?" quipped Theodore.

"Yes, I do. More to it than a silly curse, much more. But not now. I'm going to get Stanley out of that place. I know the Chief Constable, you know … play golf together! I'll be back soon."

With that, George took his leave and vanished into the night, just as fast as he had appeared .

Arriving at the police station, the sergeant at the desk immediately recognized the large shape of Lord Carberry. Standing almost to attention, he welcomed the famous figure.

"I'd like to see the Chief Constable, Sergeant."

"Sorry, Lord Carberry. The Chief Constable has already left, not half an hour ago. Is there something I can help you with?"

"Yes, Sergeant, there jolly well is. I want to know why my son-in-law is being held here. His name is Stanley Harrow."

"Your son-in-law? Well I never!" Yes sir, I'll just go and fetch Detective Inspector Russell Brown. He's the one in charge of the case. Won't be a minute, Sir, please take a seat."

The disgruntled MP paced up and down the small waiting area, grunting and groaning as he went. After a little while, the sergeant reappeared, apologizing for taking so long.

Taking Lord Carberry around the main desk, they soon came to a small office where Inspector Brown was sitting behind a paper-ridden desk.

"It's a pleasure to see you again, Sir. So sorry for the wait. I've just been talking to Mr Harrow. I must confess though, that I hadn't realized he was your son-in-law. There were one or two things that needed to be cleared up. Paper work, terrible nuisance you know."

"Yes, that may well be, but why are you holding him? Surely you don't suspect any wrong doing towards my daughter? They've just got married, don't you know!"

"Yes sir, I did understand that. Mr Harrow is, Sir, at this very moment, being released. He is simply helping us with our enquiries at this point. I really can't give you my opinion on this case, Sir. It is a very unusual set of circumstances, very unusual indeed."

"Mr Brown … Inspector… let me just say that, even if you can't see something, it doesn't mean it doesn't exist."

"Quite, Sir. In fact, I was only saying the other day to a colleague, can you see the wind? He said, of course not, but you can certainly feel it on your face and see the effect it has on the trees. You see, Sir, I tend to keep an open mind on the ways of life. Let me just assure you, Sir, Lord Carberry, I won't rest until we find your daughter, no matter where she may be."

"Yes, quite, quite, well thank you Inspector. It seems that you have your work cut out for you, so I'll be on my way." Inspector Brown stood and shook hands with his Lordship.

Stan was standing at the front desk when his Lordship came through.

"Come, my lad, we have work to do." George ordered.

They drove back to the cottage with Stan sighing over his release from captivity.

"George," Stan said with a confused look on his face. "You don't seem too surprised about what has happened. Why is that?"

"I'll tell you all that I know when we get back to the cottage. I don't want to have to repeat myself too many times with this burden."

"Well, Sir, whatever it is, I am grateful for you getting me out of that place. All I can say is that at least you all have a little faith in me."

"By God lad," George replied, "I would never have let you marry my daughter if I didn't think that you were of good intentions, eh what!"

The cottage had a certain, 'mystique', about it, as they finally arrived and got out of his Lordship's Rolls Royce. Stan noticed George was also looking at it with the same inauspicious look.

"Time is drawing close, lad!" George announced.

Stan was puzzled by this remark, but he quickly put it out of his mind when he saw Jim and a stranger walking around the outside of the cottage.

Jim noticed their arrival and stopped what he was doing. He greeted Stan and George, rubbing his hands together in the brisk, cold, night air.

"Ah, glad to see you back, Stan," said Jim. "This is Theodore, the gent I told you about. Are you ok?"

"Fine thanks. I'm glad that Lord Carberry intervened though. Hello, Theodore. What are you doing out here, Jim?"

The four men stood together while Jim explained that he and Theodore were going to use their skills as mediums to find out what spiritual activity could be found around the cottage area.

"If there is any spiritual activity around here, then, hopefully, we will be able to pick up on it. If you, Stan and of course you, George, would like to follow us, I'm sure you will both find this interesting."

"Sounds good to me," said Stan.

George mumbled something or other, but decided to go with them anyway.

"Before we start," said Jim, "it's important for us all to be protected from any evil forces. I want you to imagine that there is a strong white light above your head. Allow that light of goodness to enter through the crown of your head. Let it travel through your temple's third eye, down into your throat, into your heart and lungs. Feel this good light flow through all of your body, into your arms and legs, then outward, to form a protective shield around you. Are we okay with this?"

They all nodded in agreement, although George thought it all, 'mumbo jumbo'. "Okay then, let's start."

Theodore went slightly ahead of the group, ringing a small bell and chanting.

"What's that chap doing?" asked the astonished George.

Jim replied to him that Theodore was helping to invoke any spirits that were around. The bell, he explained, was used in many tribal cults and even monasteries around the world.

Jim stopped the group as Theodore suddenly came to a halt. Jim then stepped forward.

"I'm picking up on a male presence here." Announced Jim. "In fact, not one, but many spirits. There's anger here, my head is throbbing ... anger... the Manor, I see the Manor ... curse the Manor. This energy seems to be residual, in the soil. There were graves here! Many graves, now all gone, but for a few."

"Are you all right Jim?" asked Theodore.

"Yes, I'm all right, thanks," replied Jim. "The graves were moved from this land and these spirits seem angry about being torn away from their place of peace. They are not happy with evil sacrilege of wholesome ground. Move on Theodore, please, I seem to want to be further round the cottage."

Theodore continued his bell ringing and incessant chanting, then stopped again.

"This is the place," Jim decided. "It is pure evil. I don't like it here. It's powerful, I see entities that are not of this world... excuse me, I feel faint..."

He slumped to the ground, still conscious.

Stan and George were completely baffled at the sight that confronted then. Theodore, however, did not seem surprised at all. He had seen this sort of thing

Many times before.

Some concern arose from his Lordship as he bent down to Jim, helping him back to his feet. With Theodore's expertise, Jim soon recovered.

"Come," said Theodore, "form a circle and touch hands together. Do not let go for any reason at all. While we are like this, we are more protected and can use our combined energies to get the information we need."

Once the circle was formed, Jim once again took

up the dreaded task of contact between mortal and the spiritual worlds. The ground seemed to shake as Jim started his quest.

Fear was apparent on both Stan and George's faces.

Stan also seemed agitated. He reported feelings of hotness, perspiration covered his face.

George also felt similar feelings, which unnerved him.

"This is horrid," said Jim. "I have fire, flames ... this man is burning, he's being burnt. There's no escape, yet he seems to be laughing at his captors. The curse, he's saying the curse! I'm also picking up another person, one of good character. I'm getting the name, Tom. He's saying, 'beware the evil'. It's a warning! We must be on our guard. Wait, there's more ... he's fading, but saying, 'Time, it's time'. He's gone. Break the circle. Please gents, we'll move back inside."

They all re-entered the cottage with feelings of relief. Stan got out a couple of bottles of wine and they all sat down to talk over their experience.

"It's as I thought," Jim began, "the reason this cottage is possessed is because the remains of the man who was burnt at the stake are buried next to the back wall!"

"This is rather fascinating really," said Theodore, "because not only have we picked up on one of the actual victims of those who were burnt at the stake, but we also have this other man, who is called, 'Thomas'. If our facts are correct-and this will interest you in particular, Lord Carberry, we are talking about one of your relatives, Thomas Carberry."

"What, what?" queried his astounded Lordship, "Don't know of any Thomas Carberry, but there was one called, Thomas Beaumont. Seems you might have the names mixed up. Beaumont was a good friend of the Carberry family! so, old Thomas must have been one of the first victims then? I rather thought that."

"So that's it!" Jim assumed. "Jacks name is Carberry and not Beaumont. He must be a direct relative of yours George."

"Correct and to be precise, my elder brother, what!"

"But how does this all help us?" questioned Stan.

"Well," said Jim, "the warning of evil is prevalent anyway. We must be very careful of the way that we approach any rescue bid. If we get it wrong, then we, too, will be lost in the void of time. Also, Thomas spoke of, 'the time. I can only assume that it means that on a particular date, there will be the event of the vortex opening. That is our time for a rescue attempt."

"Good grief, man," interrupted George, "how on earth will we know when that will be?"

"I think we have that one sorted out," gleamed Theodore. "You see, according to my calculations, summer solstice was five days ago. According to the legends, satanic worshippers would perform their rituals one week before this time and then again, one week after the solstice. That means that we are at the second week in two days' time. That, gentlemen, is our only opportunity."

"Ah, yes, maybe so," sputtered George, "but there's a little more to it than that I'm afraid!"

All eyes fell upon George as he struggled to tell of his dreadful secret.

"Well, you are now all familiar with the man, Thomas Beaumont. He became a great friend of the family, while exploring the Amazon."

"Didn't he disappear through the same vortex within this cottage?" asked Stan.

"No, good gracious. Let me take you back to the times of my great grandfather, Lord Alfred Carberry. It was some years after the re-building of the village that Lord Alfred decided to build a secret tunnel between the Manor and the cottage. This was purely for reasons of escape from either place of residence, although it was more likely used to spy on the villagers. Anyway, it was when this passage was being built that Thomas became involved. You see, workers, who had been brought in from different areas, discovered a large cavern under the Manor. Thomas, being an archaeologist, was the obvious person to explore this area of unusual interest. Apparently, human remains were found, along with artefacts of a medieval origin. We still have some of these relics in the manor, damned ugly things they are too."

"I would be very interested in looking at them." said Theodore.

"Yes, indeed," mumbled George, "they are under lock and key. People say they are evil. Don't hold much with it myself, but it seems wise under the circumstances."

"Excuse me," interrupted Jim, "but why do you say that?"

"The belief is," continued George, "that they are said to hold the curse of the devil. People who disturb these relics tend to disappear or die under strange circumstances. Two workmen, that were involved with the construction of the tunnel died of a mysterious virus. No one could identify this virus because, in those days, medicine wasn't like it is now. The other thing is, Thomas suddenly disappeared while exploring the cavern. As you can imagine, all work on the tunnel and cavern was stopped, the entrance bricked up and all involved were told to keep quiet about Its existence."

"Hang on," said a puzzled Stan, "are you telling us that we have two different areas that the vortex leads to, or is it the same place or world Charlie is trapped in?"

Both Jim and Theodore looked at each other, wondering the same thing.

"Could be," said Theodore, "but there's no real way of knowing ... unless, of course..."

"Unless, of course, we explore the Manor's cavern. Is that what you are thinking, Theodore?" interrupted Jim.

"It is, but I don't believe we have the time to explore and confirm this before the vortex re-appears in the cottage."

Quietness descended upon the group, but it became obvious that George didn't look too comfortable.

Jim soon picked up on this and started quizzing him further.

"You seem a little irritated, George. There's more to this, isn't there?"

"What? Oh ... I suppose I had better tell you. The thing is, when this bomb hit the Manor back in the war, it opened up a second entrance to the cavern. I immediately had it sealed up, but it didn't stop events from happening."

"What events are we talking about, George?" asked Jim.

"Well ... one workman disappeared without trace and another had a fatal accident. Work stopped, the usual investigations took place and no one was blamed for anything. Trouble was, it took me a long time to find more contractors because word had travelled fast. They said the place was cursed. Can't blame them really."

"Is this the reason you kept the Manor quiet from Charlie?" Stan wanted to know.

"Yes, but you should understand about my own fears. I can tell you that I was in two minds over whether or not to pull the place down, let alone repair it."

"So," said Jim, "what made you carry on?"

"Good question. Well, I suppose at the end of the day, I wasn't going to be beaten by any silly curse or by something I couldn't see. One can't allow this sort of nonsense to continue. Someone has to take a stand eventually, eh, what?"

"Did anything else happen in the Manor after these tragedies?" Jim asked .

"There was some sickness. A lot of the staff kept getting sick for some reason or other. Everything seems fine now, well, except for the rumours, but I soon put a stop to that!"

"Rumours?" asked Jim.

"Oh, the usual rumours. The type that spook people after such previous talk. They talked of seeing ghosts and even objects moving by themselves. Some, they say, even disappearing completely. I must say, though, I did lose my pocket watch. Solid gold you know! Still, I had a good chat with them, told them they were imagining things and gave them a rise in their wages. That did the trick somewhat."

"Yes," said Jim laughing, "I expect it did."

CHAPTER 15

A warm, brightly lit sun, made its appearance as Charlie and Jack finished getting ready for their trek into the village.

"I've been working on some suitable clothing for you Charlie, I only had to alter them slightly." Announced Jack coming from his bedroom, holding a bundle of clothing.

"How on earth did you manage that, I never saw you doing any sewing?" Charlie said as Jack gave her the bundle.

"Did it while you slept my girl, didn't take long at all."

A long sleeved, brown jacket, fitted perfectly on Charlie's slender body, made from soft sheep's hide and dyed to obtain the correct colour for its purpose. She was then given a pair of trousers.

"Ohh, these are lovely and warm Jack," as she pulled off her pyjamas and tried them on. "How did you know my size, they fit perfectly!"

"Aye they do at that. Guesswork I suppose, but I have had a little experience before. There's one last thing though, here, try these on." Jack handed her a beautifully designed pair of leather moccasins. She soon put these on her bare feet and tied them up with strips of leather that were neatly stitched on the sides. She looked a treat as she finally put on a silver cross that hung prominently between Charlie's cleavage. She thought that it was a good idea that she still had her vest on, if only to protect her modesty. She was also given a quiver of silver-tipped arrows. They straddled her waist perfectly, hanging around her young hips.

"I look like Mrs Robin Hood." She declared to Jack, twirling her new fashion.

"You do at that Charlie," replied Jack, "better than those pyjamas, eh?"

Jack's clothing also provided a good sense of camouflage. His bow was slightly larger than that of Charlie's; made for a man's stronger hand. He also carried a silver cross around his neck. Around his waist hung a sheath that held a ten-inch, silver-bladed and bone-handled knife. Much care and workmanship had been taken with this beautiful piece of intricate, patterned carving, which extended across its whole area. A large, canvas-type bag completed his outfit.

They first worked out a plan, which would take them behind the village and come in at the back of the church.

"Are you ready then, Charlie?" Jack asked, checking that his knife was secure.

"Yep, just about, Jack."

"Okay, just follow me. We'll keep close to the hedge line, that'll keep us out of sight."

Keeping to the hedge boundaries, they arrived close

to the back of the church. They settled behind a low hedge, keeping silent and regaining their breath. The sun shone gloriously although the dew on the long grass made Charlie curse a little as she got wet on her new outfit.

"Stay here and don't move." Jack ordered. "I'm going to open the old crypt. I'll signal you to come when I'm ready and, for Heaven's sake, keep a good look out for anybody coming. If they do, whistle, like I showed you."

Whistling is one of Charlie's specialities. She learned how to, from a very young age so wouldn't find this feat an obstacle at all.

Jack sped away quickly, dodging behind gravestones and constantly searching the area for intruders. Edging closer and closer towards the crypt, he suddenly halted. His senses warned him to listen more closely. He wasn't wrong because as he stopped, he could hear voices. He glanced at the direction they were coming from, which was around the side of the building. He recognized the sound as two people talking. He froze for a moment, making sure he was concealed properly behind a gravestone.

Turning around, he noticed Charlie was lying flat by the hedge. She gave a little wave and held up two fingers to indicate she had spotted the two individuals.

Jack used his hand in a downward motion while putting his finger to his lips, suggesting to Charlie that she should keep down and quiet.

Charlie felt uncomfortable with her face pressed against the twig-strewn damp ground. It seemed that she was in this position for ages, but eventually, after some ten minutes, the two men went on their way. Jack gave a sigh of relief and carried on to the crypt entrance. The wooden door wasn't locked, but it took a bit of effort to push open because of its rusty hinges. Standing, he once again scanned the area. When he was sure everything was all right, he beckoned for Charlie to come forward.

"Flipping heck, Jack! That was a bit close for comfort, wasn't it?"

"Sure was. Come on, let's get inside, we've got to make sure there's no one else in the church."

The crypt was directly under the church, with stone steps leading the way down. A putrid odor arose as they finally walked off the bottom step. The place was very dark and damp. Charlie heard a crunch as she moved around.

"Oh my God, there are bones on the floor, I think they're human!"

"Keep it quiet, Charlie! I'm sorry about that, I should have warned you. Thing is, these monstrous people who live here just have no respect for the church, or the dead. Tread carefully. I'm just going over to the tombs. There are two large stone tombs in here. The far one contains the silver we're after. Stay where you are for a moment. I'll just check to make sure the silver is still there."

"How did it get there Jack?" she quizzed.

"I put it there some time back now, when I stole it. I got disturbed and hid it here hoping those devils wouldn't come near the place. Enough questions now."

Trembling slightly, Charlie stood perfectly still, while Jack swiftly checked the contents of the tombs.

"Its okay, the silver is still there. Now listen, Charlie, I first need to check upstairs, in the church, just to make sure that no one is prowling around. I want you to stand guard at the entrance of the tomb. Keep your ears and eyes on the job. We have to protect our escape route."

"But what if someone comes, Jack? How do I warn you?"

"Let's hope that doesn't arise. I'll only be two minutes, anyway. I won't have to go into the church itself. There's a hole in the door that I can look through. Just whistle quietly if you have to, okay?"

"Yes, master, your wish will be obeyed!"

While Jack slithered away like a noiseless snake, he thought how cheeky the young scamp was, but smiled at the thought of what a great sense of humour she had.

Charlie gently, if not cautiously, crept back towards the entrance of the dark and eerie tomb. Her thoughts started to get the better of her, thinking that the skeletons may rise up and attack her through the darkness. She lay silently by the doorway, bow and arrows placed in front of her, just in case an intruder got too close, including skeletons. All seemed quiet though.

She wondered how Jack had known the silver would still be in the same place as it had been when he came before. But then, she answered her own question. Of course, those Dronians wouldn't be able to go near the silver because they could well be destroyed themselves if they handled any of it. She wondered how Jack had managed to steal it in the first place? Another thought crept into her mind as she considered the church itself. Why would they need such a place if they were all of Satan? Surely, she thought, a church would be of no use to them, especially since it was considered to be "God's house"!

Her thoughts soon came to an abrupt end when, in the darkness, she heard a crack, as if someone had walked upon a twig and snapped it in half. Quickly, she picked up her bow, in readiness for any eventuality. Just then, a voice whispered gently across the bone-ridden floor of the tomb.

"I'm back, Charlie, how's it looking?"

"Quick, Jack, over here! I heard a twig snap. I think someone, or something, is to the right of the church."

"Could well be. I could hear voices at the front of it. Keep a sharp lookout, I'm going to get as much silver as I can, then we'll get out of here."

"Hurry then, Jack, I don't like the look of it!" Charlie warned.

Filling his sack as quickly and as quietly as possible, Jack was soon back by Charlie's side.

"Jack, there's someone moving towards us, look!"

"I see him. Keep still, he hasn't seen us yet."

With that, Jack put the bag silently down, stood in the shadows, raised his bow and let loose an arrow. The figure stumbled backwards and fell to the ground. Without hesitation, Jack pounced forward towards his victim. The silver-tipped arrow found a perfect mark right through the heart. He looked around quickly, his keen eyes piercing through the darkness. He saw no one nearby, so he ran back to Charlie.

"Come on girl, let's get out of here, they'll soon discover him!"

Picking up the bag of silver chalice cups, plates and other oddments, the couple ran towards the hedge where they came in from an opening. Without warning, an inhuman piercing scream filled the night air with dread.

"They're onto us. Quick, Charlie. Go to the end of the hedge. I'll guard your back. Keep low!"

Charlie ran as fast as she could, then struck a pose that depicted a warrior from some long lost tribe, holding the bow at the ready, while quickly checking the immediate area. Looking back at Jack, who was already busy with his bow, she noticed a figure heading her own way. Raising the silver-tipped arrow to the bow, she pulled back the string, taking careful aim and let loose. The intruder stopped suddenly, quivered, then fell to the ground. She had made her first kill with a good degree of accuracy.

At the point at which Charlie stood, she could see the main road at the end of the village. Several Dronians were running about, seeming to gather more of their folk together.

"Jack! We've got to move, a group is gathering!"

She moved a couple of yards away from the hedge with her bow raised. The bag Jack carried seemed to have a mind of its own. Suddenly, he seemed to trip over it. One of the Dronians made a run for Jack as he got up and made secure the bag. The fearsome creature got to within a few yards of him, as he struggled to pull out his knife. Then, the whistle of an arrow sliced through the air and struck the creature, straight through the heart. He fell at the feet of Jack, who was more than slightly surprised.

Regaining his senses, Jack ran to Charlie, thanking her for such a good shot. Running towards a copse of trees, they heard the sound of hoofs, racing from the village.

"There's two horsemen coming this way. Get behind the trees."

"Do you think they've seen us, Jack?"

"Not sure, but if they come too close, we'll take them."

In the distance, a vicious noise caught their attention.

"My God, Jack, do you hear that? That noise, I've never heard anything like it before in my life. It sounds almost like a wolf!"

"That's no wolf, Charlie, it's a devil dog! If it picks up our trail we're in serious trouble. Let's move, fast!"

From the end of the copse, the gallant duo headed towards the stream. An embankment of about four feet dropped down to the slow running, shallow water.

"What the hell are you talking about, 'devil dog'? What is it, Jack?"

"I haven't time for explanations, Charlie, get ready with your bow! When those two horsemen come out of the copse, we must take them out!"

The brightness of the sun suddenly appeared from behind the clouds, which gave the pair an advantage with the sun behind them. It wasn't long before the horsemen made their appearance at the edge of the tree line, bending down from their horses in an attempt to find tracks. They were still searching the same area when Jack took up his bow, aimed and fired his shot. He watched as one of the assailants fell from his horse.

Charlie too, took aim, but missed her mark. The arrow plunged its tip into the trunk of a tree. She quickly raised another arrow to her bow and felled the horse. Jack, by this time, had already taken his second shot. At the same time, the horse went down. So did the rider.

The arrow sliced the tormentor's jugular vein. Blood flew out in a torrent, like a fountain.

The pair didn't hang around to appraise themselves, but quickly hurried along the streambed, ducking and diving beneath outstretched limbs of trees, many brambles and rocks slippery with slimy moss on their protruding surfaces.

Stopping briefly, the pair, gasped for breaths of air. Through the sheer pace they had set themselves, they noticed they could still hear the sounds of mad dog and shrieks of angry evilness. Finally, they travelled about a half mile from the point of entrance to the stream.

"Sounds like they're by the stream," gasped Jack, "wondering which way to go. That devil dog can't trace our scent while we are in water."

"Well, I'm exhausted, Jack." Charlie pleaded leaning against the damp sides of the stream. "How far are we to our cabin?"

"Well, we only need to get through the quarry and about half a mile across country, and we should be safe. We'll come close to the quarry in a few minutes. Come on, those devils won't give up that easily!"

Soaked, cut and bruised, they eventually reached the point where they could depart from the stream. The noise of their pursuers seemed to have died down, or maybe it was the fact that they had lost the trail. Either way, the pair knew they were not safe yet. Struggling out of the cold water, Jack stood, only to find he was limping slightly. He took little notice as he lent his hand to Charlie, who didn't seem able to conquer the grassy slope of the stream's bank.

"The quarry is just over that hummock. Keep close now, Charlie. Once we get there, it'll be tricky."

"Jack?" Charlie asked, "why do you fear those dogs so much."

"Those devils are extremely vicious," he replied, "they're much bigger than a normal dog, more like a wolf, but with fangs that would tear you apart. I've seen one before and believe me , they are real monsters. Come on now Charlie, we've got to get moving."

Upon entering the rock-strewn quarry, they carefully climbed down the old steep pathway that had been carved out by hand, many years before.

"Jack, what was this quarry used for?" inquired Charlie.

"Oh, this place? Stone mainly, but there are several tin mines scattered around here. There's one just up in front of us actually. Hold it, quick! Get behind those boulders!"

"What is it, Jack?"

"I'm sure I heard something. Could be a trap. Back out carefully. We'll edge our way down to the quarry floor and circle around these mines."

Clambering down to a more even surface, Jack stopped behind a large rock, looking upward from where they had just stood. A great howl suddenly pierced the tranquillity of the night air as the shape of a massive animal appeared, silhouetted against the entrance of the mine from where they had just been.

"Good God, Jack, is that what you mean by a 'devil dog'? It's looking straight at us! It's enormous!"

"Hells bells!" bellowed Jack. "Quick, we must get our backs against the quarry wall. Over there will do!"

They hurried across an open space and stood with the protection of the high-sided wall behind them. The whole area had been cut into a semi-circle with small path's ringing their way around the quarry. Mainly limestone with intervals of other rock deposits, this quarry was very deep. It wasn't long before the monstrous animal appeared in the open space, some twenty yards in front of them, growling without fear as it strode towards them. Charlie and Jack raised their bows and took aim. Their arrows struck the beast with enormous force, but the beast still did not fall. Jack shouted to Charlie to reload as fast as possible. It seemed too late, as the mad dog took a gigantic leap towards them. While the beast was in flight, Jack's arrow pierced its heart and Charlie's punctured through its upper body.

The beast fell to the ground, right by their feet, still gasping and growling as if to say it was not done for yet.

Jack took no chances as he watched the extraordinary power of the dog rise up to it's feet and attempted to move upon the unsuspecting couple. . Jack took no chances as he whipped out his silver-bladed knife from its sheaf and plunged it deep into the creature's blood-oozing heart.

Its final last gasp came, but not before the beast tried to take a bite of Jack's ankle.

Charlie, seeing this grabbed a large rock, instinctively raising it high then smashed it against the creature's head. The amazing strength of Charlie made Jack quiver slightly as he saw the skull, explode into many pieces. The beast's heart, ripped out by the menace of Jacks hand, lay half on the ground and half still hanging by threads. It was finally over as they both plummeted to the ground.

"You're bleeding, Jack," Charlie noticed, "let me have a look."

"Don't fuss, woman, I'm all right, thanks to you. Check the area while I just tie up this wound. The Dronians won't be far away by now and they won't be very pleased at the sight of our work."

Charlie couldn't help but gaze down upon this amazing creature. Its head, being twice that of a lion, had a sharp pointed horn, midway along its spout. Its eyes were blood red and its teeth were like that of a sabre-toothed tiger, with a protruding large and pointed front tooth. The side teeth looked just as sharp. The body, some seven feet in length, was covered in what looked like, spiny fur. The spines, about three inches in length, stuck out as if starched by some mad person. They were those of a porcupine, but covered in a waxy fur.

Charlie thought that getting too close to this creature one would receive many wounds, just from this unusual spiny fur. The three-foot tail was of similar style, but the spines were much bigger. Its feet, if that's what they were called, were like large hoofs at the rear, while the front pair could only be derived of "fur-covered fingers" that had sharp nails at the ends. A hooked claw hung halfway down between its joints.

"Charlie! Charlie! Can you see anything?"

"Oh, sorry Jack, not at the moment, I just can't get over this creature's size." She looked around the quarry, her piercing eyes searching every nook and cranny. Hang on, what was that? I'm sure I saw something. Yes, up there, there's movement at the top of the quarry. Three, maybe. No, four. Yes definitely four figures. It looks like the Dronians have arrived!"

"Quickly then," Jack pleaded, "we've got to get out of here. Give me a hand up, will you?"

"Give me the bag, Jack," worried Charlie, "you're still bleeding quite badly."

Jack struggled to get to his feet and it soon became obvious that making the speed they needed to keep in front of the ever-nearing Dronians. Fearing that this would not be easy to achieve, they set off anyway. The sheer weight of the bag containing the silver also put a burden on Charlie's slim frame.

With little time left, Jack, using his bow as support, managed to guide them both to a small clump of trees that had an area of overgrown vegetation just in front of them. A narrow path marked an entrance towards the trees.

"Stop here, Charlie, I've got an idea to slow them down."

They stopped beyond the vegetation, amongst the trees. Jack produced a long length of string from a pouch that hung around his waist. He ordered her to tie one end to a bush, six inches above ground level, then to cover the rest of the string that ran across the pathway with leaves. He then positioned the string around another bush, some six feet away and back towards a large oak tree. It was a simple "pull and trip". trap. This could be used without notice from their pursuers.

"How many arrows have you got left, Charlie?"

"I've got six, why?"

"Good, here's the plan. I want you to climb up into that tree, hope you can climb well. Get yourself in a good position so that you can easily shoot your bow. I'll stay on the ground. I can't really climb anyway. When they come, and I believe there will be four of them, I shall give them all the encouragement they'll need, I'll trip them up with the string and then you must take out the one who is nearest your side. If I get this right, they should come at us two at a time. The path will only support two persons coming in together. You must be as quick as you can to reload your bow and take out one of the other two behind. If you don't, well let's not think about that, just do your best, okay?"

"Don't worry Jack, I won't let you down." Efficiently, Charlie scrambled up the tree with some ease

It wasn't very long before the four intruders came into view. They looked like very normal citizens, wearing the style of clothing for that period. Brandishing pitchforks, they seemed to have more energy than most folk, since their pace of speed never diminished in any way. They stopped briefly, as Jack came into their view, breaking his cover. It was enough for them to spot him. He then ran back to the cover of the trees.

They advanced rapidly as Charlie silently brought an arrow to her bow, while Jack resumed his position behind the oak tree. As he had predicted, two of the men came through the opening together. At the point where the trap lay, Jack waited with patience, then pulled the string until it became rigid. They both fell simultaneously, with a crashing thud upon the ground.

The one on the right hand side never again moved as Charlie's arrow, by this time, had already found its mark straight into his upper back. The second one soon regained his senses, but not for long, as Jack came from behind his hiding place and threw his knife with deadly accuracy towards his victim. Blood spurted out of the penetrating weapon's entrance. Try as he could, the Dronian could not pull it out. He fell back, still clutching his red-stained shirt.

The other two stopped, wondering whether to go the same way or not. Did they have the same courage as the first two? It was soon answered, as they started their own run towards Jack, who was desperately trying to pick up and load his bow. The second arrow, coming from Charlie's position, once again found its mark. The victim staggered. The arrow had gone through his heart. He then fell, howling, in front of his fellow colleague.

"Three down, one to go!" shouted Charlie with an impassionate joy.

The last survivor hurled his pitchfork towards Jack, which caused him to side step to the cover of the tree. Luckily, this man-beast had seen enough. He turned tail and ran with all his might, back the way he had come.

"Get him, Jack, quick!"

Jack really didn't need any encouragement, as he calmly walked forward and took aim at the fleeing Dronian. He must have been some hundred and fifty yards away by now, but there was no escape from Jack's accuracy. The silver-tipped arrow flew as straight as an eagle in flight. It found its prey and destroyed it.

Charlie clambered down from her hideout. She couldn't resist jumping up and down with great joy. Meanwhile, Jack had slumped down to the ground, clutching his shoulder.

"Jack! What's the matter?"

She ran to him, only to find a blood soaked shoulder.

"That damned pitch fork caught me," stammered Jack. "Find something to wrap me up, will you?"

"I'm so sorry, Jack, I didn't even see it hit you."

"I just wasn't quick enough, that's all Charlie. The thing hit the tree with one prong while the other one caught my shoulder. It'll be all right, it's only superficial."

"Superficial or not, you've lost enough blood as it is, look at your leg!"

Charlie stripped off her jacket to her undergarments. The cloth she was wearing was clean and absorbable. She had no hesitation in taking off the top that covered her beautiful, firm breasts.

"My God, girl, I wish you wouldn't do that. It could give me a heart attack!"

"Well then, at least you'll die with a smile on your face," she laughed, "now stop looking at me and keep still."

Putting her naked charms back into her jacket, she got to work on this smiling hero. With the gentleness of a young nurse, she covered his wounds with as much experience as a professional would.

A groan ascended from one of the fallen victims. Both looked around, then Charlie stood. "I'll take care of this!" she demanded.

She took one of the arrows from its case and calmly walked up to the slightly moving beast. She showed no hesitation in plunging the arrow deep into his back. In a fevered action, she made sure of its death by twisting it in even further. No more noise came from its mutilated body.

Jack was on his feet by now, and stood over the young woman's work. "For Gods sake Charlie that's enough! I think I'd better get you away from this, looks like you enjoyed it too much."

"I suppose I did, but as you would say, it's them, or us!"

Retrieving his knife from one of the victims, Jack couldn't help but wonder where Charlie got this sort of ferocity. He couldn't help thinking that he may have caused it. Charlie then decided that a stout branch would enable Jack to get around much more easily. She soon found a stout branch, shaping it, with a little guidance from her teacher. She then picked up their valuable bag of silver, and headed off towards the safety of their own, upturned world of trees.

CHAPTER 16

Stan awoke the next morning slightly the worse for wear. It seemed as if he had been on an all-night bender. The headache that he was now nursing made him search for some sort of pain relief. Theodore and Jim were already up and drinking coffee.

"Morning, Stanley," whispered Jim, "how are you feeling?"

"Not too bad, thanks, apart from a bad head. We must have put the drinks down us a bit though? It looks like we made a bit of a mess in here. Maybe the cleaner will turn up today."

"I didn't realize you had a cleaner, Stan?"

"Well, yes, Jim, at least we did have. I haven't seen her since … well, since all this business began. Come to think of it, she's supposed to come in every day. She only lives down the road. You must have seen her. Her name is Mrs Cartwright, Edna Cartwright to be exact."

"Stan," replied Jim, "I've lived here in this village for some ten years now and I've never heard of either an Edna, or the name, Cartwright."

Just then, the thunderous footsteps of Lord Carberry came down the stairs and into the room.

"Good morning, gentlemen." He looked around. "What a beautiful morning. Where's the maid service in this place? Throat's like a piece of damned sandpaper!"

"We don't have maid service, George. It looks like we don't even have a cleaner now … well, not any more, in any case."

"What are you rambling on about, young Stanley? Where's your cleaner?"

"Well, we haven't seen Mrs Cartwright since all of this happened. Maybe you could have a word with her, since she's under your employ."

"Never heard of the woman. My own maids live in at the Manor, don't you know."

"Your land manager, is his name Bill Cartwright?"

"Good grief man, no, my land manager is old Francis Fairbottom. Damn good chap too. Got an office in the Manor, eh, what."

"For Heaven's sake," Stan's confused voice spoke as he raised both his arms alarmingly, "am I going completely mad, or is it my imagination? These people came to the cottage the very first day, introduced themselves and have been working here, cleaning every day until Charlie disappeared. They said that you, Sir, had sent them to look after our needs. I tell you, they were here, in this very room!"

"Sorry, my lad, but I know nothing of these people. I've certainly not sent anyone to do your cleaning!"

"Calm down Stanley," begged Jim, "none of this adds up. Tell me, how did they look at you?"

Stan's agitation showed but he calmed down, as a chair was made available for him. "I never really took much notice of them to tell you the truth, but now, when I come to think of it, I did think that there was something odd about them. Wait though, it was their eyes, yes, I'll never forget those eyes. They were almost half closed, as if there was something wrong with them. I noticed how bloodshot they were, red, very red in fact. It was strange at the time. I mean, perhaps one person might have had some sort of medical condition, but both of them?"

"I believe," announced Theodore, "that we may have another problem."

"What? Another problem?" the great Lord of the Manor quipped, "what do you mean?

"He means, George," replied Jim, "that these two people may not be of human origin. It is possible that these people are working for the devil. In simple terms, you should understand that they could be dangerous to us. I can't tell you why they are here, or for what purpose, but make no mistake, I have never come across this phenomenon before and it concerns me greatly. Stan, did they give any information about where they live?"

"They said that they lived down the road. I'm not sure what number they live at though."

"Okay, then I think we should attempt to find out if they do, or even did, exist. I want you, Stan, to come with Theodore and myself, to check out the cottages and their occupiers. If you don't mind, your Lordship, perhaps you could return to your Manor and maybe either look at your staff list, past and present, or even cast your eyes over them. See if they look different, especially their eyes."

"Sounds a bit far-fetched if you ask me, but I suppose

the whole bloody mess is far-fetched. Still, I am of the opinion that only we, could possibly believe in all of this. I'll tell you what, by God, I'll get my daughter back, no matter what it takes!"

"Thank you, George. I'm sure that all of us in this room want nothing better to get your daughter back. Now gentlemen, we only have today to find any answers to this problem, because tomorrow is the day the vortex should open. Come on then, let's get busy."

Just then, a knock on the door took them by surprise. Stan opened it to find Detective Russell Brown standing there, with an inquisitive expression on his face.

"Good morning, Sir, oh, have I come at an inconvenient time? Never mind, I will only be a couple of minutes, if you don't mind, Sir."

"Not at all, Inspector, do come in."

The inspector entered the room and bid good morning to the rest of the gentlemen. He explained to Stan that no charges would be brought against him and that his wife had been put on the missing persons' list.

Stan sighed with relief at this news, while Lord Carberry stood up and said "I should bloody well think so too". He then went off to his business. The inspector asked Stan if there was anything he could do to help.

"I'm not sure, Inspector, what do you think, Jim?"

"I think the Inspector could be very useful to our investigation. Tell me, Mr Brown, have you ever heard of Edna and Bill Cartwright?"

"Tell you what, Sir, I was puzzled by these people when Mr Harrow mentioned them. You see, according to the electoral roll, they don't reside in these parts. This actually concerned me very much in my own investigation. It was part of the reason why I took the action I did against Mr Harrow, by keeping him at the station. Why, have you some news of them, Sir?"

"No, not really, except now we don't believe they were of human origin. We think they are of the devil-ghosts if you like, even poltergeists, but dangerous ones. In fact, Mr Brown, we are going to make a search in the village for them, by knocking doors. Would you care to come along, Sir? It would give us a lot more credibility if you could."

"It sounds very interesting, Sir. Maybe I could tag along for a short while, but after that, Sir, I think I could go one better. I have access to the archives of villagers who have lived here, in this village. Maybe that could throw some light on things. It would also serve my own ongoing investigation."

"That's marvellous, Inspector Brown, you are a great help."

"Well, Sir, I'm glad to be of assistance. There is one more thing though. Since I have a great admiration for your work as a medium, I would also like to be involved with this vortex thing. I'm sure I could be of some use and who knows, you may require an armed person be with you when you eventually get through. It would also back up Mr Harrow's story if I were present and saw it with my own eyes."

The inspector took off his raincoat, folded it over his arm then seemed to glare at each one of the group.

"You certainly make a good case, Inspector. I don't think I have a problem with you being around. What do you think, gentlemen?"

"Fine with me," said Stan noticing the others shake their heads in agreement.

"Inspector," Theodore added with a concerned look, "do you have any idea what you may be letting yourself in for? This is not going to be any picnic, you know. We are dealing with some entity that is extremely dangerous. We are entering a world of the unknown. We really have no idea about what to expect once we enter this kingdom."

"Sir, if you knew my wife, you would fear nothing. No, I am fully aware of the consequences, but I have to find these things out for myself. It would be a great thrill for me to work with such distinguished company. Oh, and by the way gentlemen, perhaps you could drop my title and use my name, Russell."

They all laughed and agreed to him taking part.

"By the way, Russell," queried Jim, "what type of gun will you bring with you?"

"Oh just standard issue, why?"

"Well, we should all be aware by now that silver is probably our best defence against these creatures. If you could lay your hands on some silver bullets, it would afford us with a unique weapon. I'm not sure where you might be able to obtain some from though?"

"I see what you mean Sir." Stroking his chin in thought, Russell continued. "Tell you what, leave it to me, I'll see what I can do."

The foursome split into two groups, Stan with Theodore, and Jim with Inspector Russell. They wandered down the road, knocking at each door, asking questions. It soon became obvious that no one knew of the mysterious Edna and Bill Cartwright, except for one old resident. He thought he recognized the name, but could not give any details. It was at this point that Russell Brown decided to head off and check the archives. The other three went back to the cottage to make plans for the forthcoming events.

That evening, when all five were present, discussions seemed very tense. An atmosphere of foreboding seemed imminent.

"Well," began George, "I'm more confused now than when I started. According to the employment list, Edna Cartwright is one of the in-house maids. This chap, oh yes, William Cartwright, I suppose he's called, 'Bill', for short, anyway, he's some sort of land manager on my payroll. Dashed if I know, never heard of them myself. These people have not been seen by any of my staff, let alone heard of them. I should also say that they've never taken any wages. Well, damn it gents, who in their right mind, wouldn't take their wages, eh, what? It seems like no one else has ever heard of them."

"Ah yes, indeed," said the intrepid Detective Russell Brown, "and it is with little wonder. My investigations have revealed that Mr and Mrs Cartwright were villagers here, in," he flicked through his notebook that he had in his inside jacket pocket, "1807. There are no records of their deaths, in either this county or the surrounding areas. It seems, gentlemen, that they simply vanished. I have to say, however, that records are quite poor in their documentation, and so I took it upon myself to probe further. I went to the next village from here, Myston, which is not far away. After talking to the local priest there, he produced a very large book of documentation.

According to these parish records, I found something very interesting. One particular passage recorded that, 'unknown interred persons were received by this parish, in the 18th century'. The dates were unfortunately unrecognisable. So, gentlemen, you will have to make up your own minds about this couple, but all I can say to you is that I believe they did indeed once live in these parts, many, many, years ago."

"Thank you for that, Russell," Jim said. "I'm glad you're on our side with the experience you have. And thanks to you too, George. I have to say that I'm not very surprised by what I hear. It is what I would expect. I can say to you, Stan, that you haven't imagined it, these people were in your house, even though they are not now of this world. In fact, I would say that they have the ability to come and go from one world to another. They are on a particular mission, probably to lure victims through the vortex and into the clutches of Satan's angels. For what purpose, I'm not too sure as yet. But in my opinion, something is extremely wrong and may well affect us humans in a sinister way. We need to be on our guard at all times though, gents, since we are dealing with something that is very unusual and, even more, very dangerous. Theodore, would you like to explain what we will be doing tomorrow?"

"Okay," began Theodore moving around the room, "but first you should notice that I have placed a large silver cross by the wall where the vortex opens." He points to the place in question. "This is for our protection this evening, just in case anything tries to come through. Now, tomorrow we will place several silver crosses around in a semi-circle at exactly 12 noon, by the wall where the vortex will appear."

"This vortex thing," interrupted George, "how can you be sure that it will open at 12 noon?"

"Well, that is a good question, George, but you will have to trust me on this one. I have done the research on Satanical rituals and it seems to be the trend, that in those days these events always began at midday. Okay?"

"Hmmm, yes, maybe you have something there, you're the expert old chap, eh," George pondered.

"Right then. Four of us will go through the vortex when it first appears, with one person standing guard on this side. I think you would best suit this task, George. We will need someone who is very strong and has the ability and experience of an officer. We will need this type of person in case we get into any difficulties. Another point though, George, Charlie will be the first one out. It is important that she will need to see a familiar face. So, what do you think then, George?"

"What, what? Strong you say, officer? I suppose I am that. Very well, you can all rely on me gentlemen, but I tell you now, if I think things aren't going to plan, then I shall burst into this er ... vortex thing and rescue her myself!"

"Exactly George, your attributes precede you. That's why we have picked you. It is possible that we may well have to come out fast, so when we do, make sure we are clear of the circle, then move the crosses towards the opening, lined up in a straight line, next to the wall and then replace the large cross behind. This will stop any intruders from entering. Is that quite clear, George?"

"Yes, nothing will get through me I can assure you of that!"

"Thank you. Jim, would you like to ask anything?"

"Yes. Russell, have you had any luck with the silver bullets?"

"Indeed. I will pick them up from my man, at ten o'clock tomorrow morning."

"That's excellent. We will, of course, all be wearing the silver crosses for our own protection. Once inside, these, gents, may well be the one thing that will keep you safe, so wear them round your neck in full view." Theodore pass's around the silver cross's from his bag.

"So how long will you be in this other world?" George asked.

"I can only surmise that it will be minutes, rather than hours, or even days. We are talking of a time zone, one place that is there, but isn't on our own time line. In simple terms, time will probably stand still for you, George, making it seem as though we go in and then come out. For us, however, time will go as normal for that period. I hope that this makes sense, it is a difficult thing to explain. Right then, gentlemen, I'll continue. The only other item left is these knives."

Jim then reached for a holdall from beside him. It contained several items including books, compass and, of course, three silver bladed knives. They were about ten inches in overall length. A marvellous white-boned handle had been handcrafted and embellished with a scrolled pattern along its edges. Various symbols of a religious nature covered the centre section, which showed the tribe's unique nature. The sharp blades were covered in a protective moulding of straw. They shone so brightly that a person's face could be seen in them. In fact, they looked as if they had just been made.

"These were a gift to me for work I did in western Africa. They were a symbol of good over evil. They were used in rituals, of the Mombazala tribe. I have the proper cases in here for them. Ah, yes, here they are. Please keep them within these, we don't want any accidents."

"Goodness," squawked the Inspector, "those things are lethal, I hope you don't have to use them!"

"Don't worry, Russell, they're just another precaution. We don't know what to expect in there, so better be safe than sorry."

With that, the inspector bid them goodnight, followed by Lord Carberry, who needed to return to the Manor for his wife. She had been staying there under his Lordship's instructions. It was felt that there was little she could achieve by moping about around the cottage. The truth, however, was that George didn't want her involved too much, because of her slightly nervous disposition, along with her panic attacks. She had, however, been kept informed of all main events.

CHAPTER 17

Jack rested well that evening. Charlie had cleaned his wounds and re-dressed them. After a well-deserved meal that she cooked, consisting of duck with pignuts, plus a delicious herb sauce, they sat around, chatting.

"We have to be up early tomorrow morning, Charlie. There's a lot to do. You do realize that tomorrow's the day, don't you?"

"It went out of my mind, to tell you the truth, Jack, There's been so much happening just lately."

"Yes, time passes very fast here, but I'm glad for that. It will be nice to get out from this hell hole."

"Okay, Jack," asked Charlie leaning forward on the table with some eagerness, "so what's the plan?"

"When we get up, I want you to prepare the clay for the mouldings. I think that we will need these extra cross's for our plan to succeed. I'll get the furnace going and start melting down the silver. We must have this all finished well before mid-day. The procession from the village will arrive at the cavern by this time. I know of a good hiding place, close to the wall where the vortex will open. We'll wait there until the Dronians are well into their ritual, sneak out quietly and lay down the crosses, in

124

a semi-circle. We have to be within this semi-circle before any of these monsters realize it. The rest, hopefully, will go according to plan. Hopefully, we will be rid of this place and we'll be out of here permanently, okay?"

"You make it sound so simple. But what if we are discovered too early?"

"Then plan B will take effect. No, we won't run, that probably wouldn't work. We'll have to fight, girl, and fight hard. I'll defend the area with my bow and arrows. You, my beautiful niece, must, at all costs, continue to finish the half circle until it is impossible for them to cross it. We simply have to work fast for this to succeed. Any more questions?"

"You may need me to help with keeping them at bay!"

"No, you must only concentrate on one thing. In any case, you won't have your bow with you. You'll need both hands on the crosses. Remember, without this circle of silver, they can still come after us through the vortex. That's why you will need to go through the opening and lay the rest of the crosses on the other side. That's vital if we are to free ourselves."

Charlie looked rather frightened, but knew Jack was right. After all, she owed her life to him for saving her from certain capture when she entered this satanic world.

The day had been tough on both of them, particularly Jack, after all, he was no spring chicken. They both retired to their separate bedrooms and were soon fast asleep.

Dawn broke early the next morning, but this didn't seem to bother Jack, who was already outside, stoking his furnace. It wasn't long after that Charlie had also arisen. It was as if she had woken up to an alarm clock ringing. She had no idea what time of day it was, but she didn't seem to care. It was a beautiful, sun-struck morning. She noticed the smell of firewood burning and wondered if she had actually overslept.

"Oh, my God," she whimpered, "I'm supposed to be helping Jack."

Suddenly the door burst open to reveal the smiling man himself.

"Ah, morning Charlie, sleep well?"

Jack had just opened the door to come back in and find, to his amusement, that she was stretching her arms out like the wings of a beautiful dove.

"You're a wondrous sight, that's for sure. The pot is boiling, fancy a nice cup of tea?"

"Sorry Jack, I should have been up earlier. Yes, thanks, I'd love one."

Sitting down together, they drank tea and demolished what was left of a rabbit stew. "A good breakfast will set you up for the day." Charlie decided that Jack's quote rang true, for all people.

It wasn't long before they were both outside, attending to their different tasks. Charlie was thoroughly enjoying herself with the clay moulds. She found it great fun imprinting the cross in the damp clay. One mould would take three imprints. After she had done the imprinting, she placed a very flat layer of clay on the top, then bored a small hole in which the silver would be poured. This was all done in a wooden box, which kept everything in place. When all of the silver had been melted and the moulds filled, the pair could relax for a little while, until the silver had set. About half an hour later, Jack gave Charlie the pleasure of breaking open the moulds. She smiled joyfully as she took the moulds from the box. Then, with a hammer, and a hard-hitting blow, the clay shattered like a china tea set. It revealed the beautiful silver crosses, which glistened brightly in the streaks of sunshine that poured down through the trees. After a good cleaning, they were put into a sack bag that would eventually be hung around the strong shoulders of Jack.

Time was now starting to draw close and they knew it was now or never. Gathering their weapons together, they started the short journey towards the cave entrance. The sun was warm as they sped with all haste across the fields. It appeared very quiet which was good for them, because they knew they had arrived there before the procession did. Still, Jack continued to scan the whole area, particularly the closing area of the cavern.

"It's just over this small ridge, Charlie, keep close to me."

"Don't you worry, Jack. I'm frightened enough as it is!"

The entrance was dark and uninspiring, with rocks that were scattered to the sides of the walls. A slimy algae centre path, trickled with water, as it found its way down its journey into the cavern. It felt too quiet as they made their way but Jack had an awful sense of foreboding, but it never seemed to affect Jack's manner. His strong character never wavered, not even when he stopped Charlie in her tracks, did he seem to worry. "Stand still for a minute. I can see a light just ahead."

"What do you think it is, Jack?"

"Ah, it's okay; it's the light of the main cavern. Come on!"

Stopping at the vast interior of the cavern, Jack pulled Charlie behind a large boulder, just inside the entrance. He scanned the whole cavern for signs of life, particularly by the glistening, stone altar. When he was satisfied, they moved quietly across the floor, staying behind the cover of fallen rocks, until they came to a small opening behind a large boulder. About two feet above the ground surface and about six feet in width and height, going backwards to about ten feet, the rock hid the small hideout, which gave a good panoramic view of the whole interior of the cavern.

"Right, we've got to be silent from now on. Get a good handful of the crosses and keep them in your hand. We have to be ready for when I say to go. I'll come out first and cover you, then you must be as fast as possible to get those crosses laid out in a semi-circle. The vortex will appear to the left of us, where this wall is flat. You must start and finish with the crosses, to enclose the whole area of the vortex. Okay?"

"Yes, I've got it, Jack, how long will we have to wait?"

"Not long, in fact, not very long indeed."

She gazed around the huge space that surrounded them, noticing the redness of the high ceiling, which was lit up by burning lanterns that were deposited around the walls and by the altar. A large upstanding stone, to the right of the altar, had the manacles attached that Jack had described earlier. Sending a quiver up her spine, she realized what that particular area was for. As she gathered several crosses into her hand, she heard a low chanting. It seemed that it was coming from the main entrance. It was at this time that Charlie wished she had her bow and arrows. She realised though, that Jack was right in not allowing her to bring it because she wouldn't have been able to lay the crosses and help Jack at the same time.

"Here they come girl, be ready!"

A procession of hooded, monk-like people then appeared at the cavern's entrance. Led by a tall Dronian, he carried a wooden staff that had several bells attached to it. Another person who carried a large jug by a string handle closely followed him. These two headed for the flat wall, close to where Jack and Charlie lay hidden. The rest of the procession came into view, including a beautiful girl adorned upon a chair, supported by two long lengths of timber carried by four of the hooded figures. A rosette of flowers adorned her head. A skimpy outfit, which barely covered her fresh young body, was set off with a rosette of flowers. Her long golden hair flowed beautifully down her back. This part of the procession went by the altar, where the girl was put down and taken to a high-backed, stone throne. She didn't move, as the robed figures removed her carrying chair to the side of the wall. They then encircled the altar.

The chanting grew louder as the lead man, the high priest, banged his staff upon the floor three times. He chanted Latin verses as the priest's assistant strolled around him, splashing the contents of the jug upon the wall surface. He then went back behind the priest, who was holding up the staff towards the wall. The wall started to glow in a greenish, yellow aura. Within minutes, it settled down to its usual rounded shape. Once this was done, the vortex now opened, the two figures went to the altar and took up their positions. The high priest stood at the one end of the altar, then put the staff he was holding on the top. The chanting grew louder as the high priest raised his hands, then, bringing them down, he joined hands with the rest of the hooded Dronians.

Charlie noticed a hollow in the wall of the cavern, just to the right of the main entrance. Within its hollow, she could clearly see lots of skulls, one on top of each other. Skeletal remains were also scattered across the floor. This made her shiver, as she thought of all of the victims who were sacrificed before and what this poor, unsuspecting young girl would have to go through. She considered that she must have been drugged or maybe put into a deep trance. Then, looking at Jack, she noticed how his face seemed to boil with anger. He was not enjoying what he was seeing. He kept a watchful eye though, on the positions of the many Dronians.

"Jack, can't we do something for that poor girl?" she whimpered, touching his arm lightly.

"Doubt it. We have to think of ourselves first. Tell you what though, if I get the chance, I'll put an arrow in her chest. I'm sorry Charlie, but believe me, it's better than what she would get if I don't. Be ready now. A few more minutes, then the Satanicals will appear. Just keep calm when they arrive, they're not a pretty sight."

At that moment, vapour rose from the altar's surface. It grew stronger, turning from a yellowish colour into more of a green. It continued to form into a dense mass.

Without warning, a deep, ear-piercing sound echoed a tremendous howling. It erupted from the altar, along with a putrid stench. A large shape could now be made out from within the vaporous mass. It appeared to be that of a wolf, although much bigger, closer to the size of a small horse. The misty vapour, which had an awful stench of rotted flesh, dissipated itself all around the cavern. There stood the most grotesque creature imaginable. As it stood upright, the creature's hind legs took on a more human form, but much larger, with claws that stretched out like sharpened knives. Brown fur covered its body, while its enormous thick muscular arms showed off its 'bear-like' claws. Its head, covered in fur, resembled that of a lion's mane. The nose also seemed to be of a lion, although the general structure did have humanoid characteristics. Two very sharp pointed teeth, one each side of its mouth, gave the impression that it could easily rip through flesh. A single horn, protruding from its forehead, boasted a razor-sharp, serrated edge.

With ease, the creature jumped from the altar, easily missing the chanting Dronians. It stood, looking at the girl, deciding if she was a worthy sacrifice. He gave a rapturous howl, then raised his arms towards the altar. Within minutes, two more Satanicals appeared from the altar. Although slightly smaller, their aggression showed they were just as powerful. They quickly jumped off the altar, one taking up a position near the main entrance. The second one headed off towards the back of the throne. These were the guarding beasts, serving their master.

The devil leader screeched out its commands to the Dronians. It commanded them in a weird type of Latin.

They obviously knew what he meant because, without delay, these hooded figures walked towards the girl, picked her up, then stood her by the manacled stone. It was here that they ripped off her clothing and chained her to the shackles. An awful event seemed likely to happen, but she still looked calm, as if she wasn't really there. Her eyes were almost fixed upwards, as the Dronians ripped off her clothing. Taking off their own robes, still chanting, they then formed a circle around the girl. The high priest stepped forward and savagely raped her.

Charlie gave a gasp, almost dropping the crosses in her hand, but luckily Jack managed to put his hand over her mouth to quiet her. He gently whispered into her ear.

"I know it's awful, but please keep quiet. Our lives depend on it. This is just the beginning, there's a lot worse to come."

CHAPTER 18

Stan, Gentle Jim, Theodore, Detective Russell Brown and Lord Carberry were in the final stages of their preparation. The silver crosses had been laid into a half circle, protruding from the wall of the lounge. They were finally ready to go through the vortex, which was now open.

"Before you go, gents," his Lordship said, "I have brought you something that you may find useful."

His Lordship produced a long holdall, not unlike one that fishermen would use to carry their fishing rods. Unzipping it, he produced three spears, each four feet in length, with silver tipped heads.

"Good grief," said the surprised detective, "where on earth did you get those from, the Zulu's?"

"As a matter of fact, yes, I did. Well, I acquired them from a trip to Africa. Got the shields at the Manor, but I didn't think you would need those, eh, what?"

Theodore took one and examined it.

"My God," he explained, "these are ceremonial spears! Only this particular type has the solid silver blades. I would say that they could come in very handy. Thank you, your Lordship."

"Ah, yes, do try to bring them back, won't you? Quite like the things myself."

Keeping one for himself, Theodore gave the other two spears to Stan and Jim. The detective was quite happy with his handgun, complete with silver bullets. The four men were now fully armed. They started to walk into the area of the vortex. Russell and Jim went in first, followed by Stan and Theodore.

The shock scene that greeted them took them by surprise. Seeing naked persons, all men, surrounding a young girl, with one raping her, chained up like a dog, made them feel physically sick. They noticed the horrid animal-like creatures, and gasped at their monstrous form. The abrupt scenario completely took Jack and Charlie by surprise. They had just started to make their way down from their hiding place. Jack automatically raised his bow towards these new invaders, then realized they were friendly. Charlie couldn't believe her eyes.

"Stan, Stan! It's me, Charlie!" She shouted out unwittingly.

The two groups looked at each other, but so did the Satanical guards, who were by now, bounding their way towards them. Quick as a flash, Jack reacted. He aimed his bow at the nearest beast, letting loose an arrow. It found its mark in the chest of the guard who had come from the main entrance. The beast staggered back for a moment, then regaining his ferocious strength, continued towards them.

Jack shouted to Charlie to keep on going towards the vortex, while he reloaded for another shot.

Stan saw what was happening and ran to help her.

"Get the crosses laid, Charlie, quickly!" Jack bellowed as loudly as he could.

Stan dropped his spear and pulled her towards the vortex. They then started laying out the many crosses.

Meanwhile, the injured guard reached Jack, who had his knife out, ready for his encounter with the beast. He hadn't time for another shot with the bow, so dropped it and reached for his knife. Time and time again, Jack plunged the knife into the beast, realizing just how strong the creatures really were. He kept thinking to himself that these were no ordinary animals and that it could take more strength than he could muster. He wondered if his own time was finally up.

It took a second man, Russell, who had worked his way around the back of the creature, to help rescue him. Time and time again, Russell struck hard, hitting the beast over the head with his gun. It didn't seem to make much difference, although it did turn its head for a second. With putrid blood spilling everywhere, it managed to bury its claws into Jack's shoulder, then, with his body, the creature pushed Russell backwards. This action stunned the detective as he hit the floor with a thud. The Satanical claws were still embedded into Jack's shoulders as it renewed its attack on his now, almost defenseless victim.

Jack could not resign himself to this sort of death so, with every ounce of energy he had left, he managed to head-butt his assailant with great force. The Satanical let go of Jack's shoulders and stepped back. A shot from Russell's handgun echoed around the cavern as it struck the creature in its head. It sent the wild beast sprawling across the floor, blood raining out, staining a large area. Finally over, the creature lay dead.

Russell then turned his attention towards the group, who were desperately trying to keep some sort of order. Without hesitation, he fired another shot. This time, it was aimed at the second Satanical, who pounded towards Jim. The bullet missed, but Theodore quickly threw his spear, like he had done this his whole life. It hit the creature in its side. Jim then thrust his spear into the neck of the beast. It reeled back, but not for long, as it pulled both spears out and threw them on the floor with contempt.

Russell was in no position to shoot at the beast again for a certain shot, because both Jim and Theodore were too close to it.

The Dronians advanced upon the group as Russell, making his way back towards them, started to shoot them down. At least this was successful.

"The girl, free the girl!" shouted Charlie.

Little could be done at this point. The men, apart from Stan, were too busy holding back the second Satanical. Then Jim shouted to Stan. "Get me one of the crosses, Stan, then get one to our friend. Hurry!"

Charlie had, with the help of Stan, just completed the semi-circle, so Stan told her to stay within this area. He quickly retrieved two of the crosses and sprinted across the floor to Jim and Theodore, who were struggling to keep back the dreaded creature. Stan quickly handed over the two crosses. Jack reprieved Theodore gently pushing him back in order to gain a better position. Both Jack and Jim held the crosses out in front of them, until they were face-to-face with the horrid beast. This seemed to work, as the Satanical fell backwards, screaming with pain.

Jim followed the creature down to the floor and placed the cross onto its chest. The Satanicals time was up as a burning smell of flesh arose in plumes of vile-smelling smoke.

Theodore looked for Jack, who had fallen to the floor through the loss of blood. He rushed to Jack's aid picking him up and half dragging him into the circle. Charlie then shouted to them. "My God, that animal has started moving! Theodore, watch out!"

"I see it!" replied Theodore quickly letting loose of Jack.

He changed course, heading towards the half-erect beast.

Theodore kicked him back down, thrusting the cross into its chest.

The effect was the same, more obnoxious smoke filling the air, the silver cross burning through its chest.

"Look out!" cried Russell, as the leader of the Satanicals came pounding over towards them.

"Get back into the circle!" shouted Jack, "everybody hold their cross up, quickly!"

Stan got back in the circle, after first helping Theodore and Jack. They all then formed a shield of silver, with the crosses held out in front of them.

The monstrous leader of the Satanicals came towards the circle of protection with a fury, stopping close by. Peering down at his comrade's disintegrating bodies, he emitted a high-pitched howl. He raised himself upwards, arms held out, and in a gruff-sounding voice said, "You shall not escape me, I promise you!"

"Wanna bet?" laughed Theodore.

"Stan, get Charlie out, now!" said Jim.

"No!" she yelled back, "we can't leave the girl. Do something!"

"Look towards the cave entrance, there's even more Dronians coming!" shouted Jack. "We've got no chance of any rescue."

"It's the Cartwrights!" added Stan.

"We've got more company than those," rattled Jim. "There's more devils, coming from the altar!"

"Sorry, Charlie," said Jack, "nothing we can do for the girl. My bow is over there, out of reach."

"Russell, you still got some bullets?" asked Theodore.

"Yes!" he said checking his gun.

"Then for Heavens sake, shoot the girl!"

Russell glanced at the group and, after seeing the agreeing nods from them, and also seeing the advancing beast, he drew his gun, took aim and shot the girl, dead center in her forehead.

Stan pushed Charlie through the vortex, then followed. Her father, who quickly brought her out of the circle of crosses, greeted her with great surprise. The rest of the team followed. Without hesitation, George replaced the large cross in front of the vortex and then re-laid the crosses in a straight line along the path of the vortex.

The vortex's image started to change and it became almost transparent. The team could easily see through the wall into the cavern from where they had come. The vile creatures were close to the half circle of crosses, not daring to go any further. More and more were led in by the Cartwrights. It seemed only a matter of time before one of the Dronians would have been sacrificed to remove the silver crosses. The vortex then dissipated and all was back to normalcy.

No sound came from the wall. It appeared to be over.

The jovial Charlie was busy cuddling her husband, Stan, while the rest of the group was questioning Jack. It seemed everyone was happy with the outcome, except Detective Russell Brown. He pondered his thoughts about how he could put in his report about the whole venture, but decided no one would believe him anyway.

"Gentlemen," interrupted Gentle Jim, "oh, and of course, Charlie. I don't want to be a party pooper, but unfortunately, our work has not been completed yet."

"Eh, what," muttered George, "what are you talking about? Surely we have done what we set out to do. My daughter is safe, Jack has been rescued, the vortex has disappeared, what more do we need?"

"I think," said Theodore, "that before Jim and I tell you more that we should see to our wounds, get something to eat, then sit down, discuss what we have been through, then get on with the job in hand. Do you agree, Jim?"

"Yes totally. A good clean up, rest and then the debriefing. If anybody needs stitching up, we'll get that sorted first. Stan, you seem to have a few wounds, get Charlie to check them out. Jack, you may need a complete medical. By what I see, I think you need to be checked by a doctor."

"I'll not disagree with you there, my man!" Jack painfully said.

"I'll go along with that," said George. "We don't want our eldest and most important person to be flagging out on us. I'll take you straight to my doctor's. I'll have no arguments, old chap.eh. You've been through enough!"

"Okay, okay, I know when to surrender, bless you, George."

"Russell," continued Jim, "I think you need to pop along as well. The beast that attacked you must have left its mark. I have to say, Russell, that your bravery certainly inspired the rest of us. How on earth did you manage to recover so quickly? When you were flung back to the floor, you fired off two rounds in quick succession. You deserve a medal and if I could give you one, I would!"

"Indeed, yes indeed. I was only doing my job, though. Most interesting, I must say, most interesting. I suppose I could come along to the doctor's. I can give some verification that I am a detective investigator, say that it was police business, if anyone asks awkward questions." The quick thinking detective embarrassingly said. "I think maybe we should keep this incident to ourselves, for the time being, anyway."

"Good thinking," replied Jim, "we don't need awkward questions just yet. There's more to come, gents, so please, get yourselves sorted first. Okay everybody, this place is still unsafe to stay here. We'll go to my cottage for the time being, then, when those who need treatment have returned, I suggest George, if you don't mind, that we make our way to the Manor for de-briefing and the final venture. Has anybody got any questions?"

"Fine with me, old chap," said George, "but I think we should get some other clothing for Jack. He looks like Robin Hood in all that gear, as does my own daughter, eh, what?"

"I'll get you some of my stuff, Jack, okay? Come upstairs and we'll sort something out for you," Stan insisted. "You'd best do the same when Jack has changed Charlie!" They then went upstairs. Charlie shylessly agreed, but looked sheepishly at the now quiet group of all males.

"Er, if you don't mind… well, I haven't seen Stan for ages, I wonder if...?"

"It's all right Charlie," Jim laughingly smiled, as did the others, "we understand. I have a lovely spare room for you and your husband to catch up. I'm afraid it's only temporary though, a few hours at the best. Okay?"

"I didn't mean that we would … you know...!"

Everyone burst into rapturous laughter, but at least they realized that husband and wife needed time alone, especially after what they had been through.

CHAPTER 19

Stan and Jack reappeared from upstairs. Jack looked more modern wearing some of Stan's clothes, but he left off his shirt fearing that he would get even more blood on it. The dressings were soaked, but atl least the bleeding had now stopped. The rest of the group seemed to be in a joyous mood, still laughing at Charlie's remarks..

"What's all the laughter about?" asked Stan.

"It's nothing, Stan," an embarrassed, Charlie said. "My goodness, Jack, you look quite trendy! I'll get you a towel to cover your top."

"Maybe, but you Charlie, look like Robin Hood's assistant. Perhaps you might like to change into something a little bit more modern?"

"Yes, you're right. Won't be a minute."

Before the last of the group had dispersed to their various tasks, Jim recommended that a large cross should be hung on the wall, where the vortex had originated. This, he said, would help prevent the vortex from re-opening and letting in unwanted neighbours. Stan soon found a hammer and a nail, then proceeded to put up the largest cross they could find.

His Lordship had, by now, taken Jack to his private

doctor to get treatment. Detective Inspector Russell Brown went with them.

Charlie grabbed a quick bath, then joined Stan, Theodore and Jim, as they all proceeded to Jim's cottage.

Jim's cottage, although a lot smaller than Stan's and Charlie's had a typical, yet intricate, patterned design work English thatched roof. The thatch hung only a couple of feet from the doorway. Rambling roses covered the ancient structure of an archway that showed off its picturesque beauty. Upon entering the doorway, a very comfortable living room was adorned with a magnificent open fireplace with a large mantelpiece set above it. Cark wooded oak beams straddled whitened walls.

"What a beautiful little cottage this is. Have you lived here for long?" asked Charlie.

"About ten years. But let us first introduce ourselves. My name is Professor Jim Hawkins. Folk around here call me Gentle Jim. I expect that it's due to my nature. Anyway, my close friend and dear colleague is known as Theodore Philips. I'm sure you will find him very interesting, but I'll let him tell you all about himself. I am what you might call a spiritualist medium. In other words, I can naturally contact and speak with past, spiritual beings. I work part-time at the university as a parapsychologist, researching psychic phenomena. I've also written a couple of books on the subject. Now, is there anything else I can tell you?"

"Wow, what an introduction and what a fascinating person you are. Thank you, Professor, for now anyway. Theodore, are you a professor as well, and, if you don't mind me asking, what country do you come from?"

"Ha, ha wondered when we would get to the colour bit."

"Oh, sorry, I didn't mean...."

"Its fine, Miss Charlie, I don't take offence to my race. I have been in this country for fifteen years now, but I was born in Africa. My parents died tragically from a terrible disease. After that, I came to England to study history of the ancient worlds. I graduated in 1968 with a PhD. I have spent many years researching ritual aspects of the many tribes around the world. I also work with archaeologists to determine certain finds that often come to light. I am here though to assist Jim and yourselves, to free you of these dreadful violations that come from within the paranormal world. I have, like Jim, also written a book on my many discoveries."

"Well, gentlemen, you are the most interesting, distinguished, and, may I say, brave people I have ever met. I can't thank you enough for what you have already done. But you say it isn't over yet, why?" enquired Charlie.

"I'd rather wait for the other chaps to get back first," Jim said. "That way, I won't have to repeat myself."

"Okay, that's fair enough. One thing I would like to know, though, who is this detective and what is he doing here?"

"I think I'd better answer that one, Charlie," said Stan. "The detective, Inspector Russell Brown, became involved when I reported you missing. It was hard work trying to convince the police officers at the station about your disappearance. They didn't believe me at first. In fact, they must have thought I was some sort of lunatic, escaped from an asylum, or something. Anyway, after I found some documents and a book in our bedroom at the cottage, I came across the name of a local medium who lived in our own village. He's sat here, oh by the way my many thanks, Jim. I approached him, or should I say, flung myself at him and he agreed to help me.

"Crikey," continued Stan brushing back his hair with both hands, "this is worse than being interviewed by the detective! Still, I'll carry on. A few days passed Charlie, when I was summoned to the police station. Apparently, my past in Australia cropped up and I was then a suspect to some sort of murder."

"Oh Stan, you poor thing, how awful!" said Charlie giving him a quick hug.

"Yes, it was. I even had to endure the inside of a cell! That wasn't very pleasant either. So, anyway, your father turned up, spoke to the Detective Inspector, and the next thing I knew, I was out of there."

"Well that should have been that, surely?" she said with an alarmed expression. "So how come this Detective join the happy band of ghost busters?"

They all laughed at the thought of being what Charlie described them as: ghost busters. When everyone had quietened down, Stan took up where he left off.

"I'm not too sure about why he decided to help us out, but I can tell you, he was and still is, a very valuable member of our group. We could have been in serious trouble if he hadn't been there! It seems though our Mr Brown likes to finish a job he's working on, no matter how far he has to go. Maybe you should ask him yourself?"

"Yes, I think I will. You'll have to forgive me, I've

never heard of any police officer getting involved in such a bizarre case before. Now, Mr Hawkins, would you mind awfully if Stan and I could have a little time together?"

"Of course, you deserve it. If you go through that door over there, you should find it quite comfortable. We'll let you know when the others get back, ok?"

"Thanks so much. Come on, Stan, I think that we have some catching up to do."

Stan's red face confirmed his embarrassment but eagerly went with his wife. Once inside the cosy room , Charlie noticed that Stan seemed to be in a world of his own. Asking what the matter was, he replied with a distant expression.

"It's nothing really Charlie," he murmured, "I just can't seem to get rid of my fears."

"Fears," Charlie quizzed, "what fears?"

"oh gosh," he thought, "it just seems that my past has caught up with the future. I feel I'm being haunted continuously not only by the past, but by what's going on now. I thought that I'd lost you Charlie; I couldn't bear the thought of that. You're my most precious love. Oh God Charlie, when will we finally be like everyone else, free, happy and most of all, secure in our home!"

"Oh Stan, you have been through so much. I do understand my darling, but there's nothing that we can do about the past. Try not to worry my love, all of this will soon be over and we can settle down to a beautiful life together. Now com on, we've got some catching up to do!" Charlie grabbed hold of Stan and pushed him onto the unused bed. She jumped on top of him, kissing him like a teenager.

About an hour afterwards, the rap on the door sounded the return of the other three unlikely heroes. Charlie and Stan re-appeared from the spare bedroom with flushed faces. Little notice was taken from the others.

"Glad to have you back, gents." Greeted Jim. "Everything go okay?"

"Thanks Jim yes. No problems. A couple of stitches, needles for both of us and some smelling salts." Jack laughed at this point, turning around to look at the embarrassed Russell Brown.

"Sorry, what was that," grinned Theodore, "smelling salts?"

"Well, I'm rather afraid they were for me," said the detective, "I never could stand needles. I think I must have passed out. Sorry, gents."

"Oh, don't apologize." Jim's voice echoed between fits of laughter. "It happens to the best of us."

Detective Brown saw the funny side of his embarrassment and joined in with everybody's humour. The group seemed to be possessed by this incident. Once the laughter had diminished, they all set off for the Manor.

Mildred spotted the cars rolling up the main driveway. When she noticed Charlie in the front seat of her father's car, she quickly made her way to the front door and ran out to meet them.

"Oh, Charlotte, thank heaven you're safe! I thought I'd never see you again, oh, my dear darling, what you must have been through."

"I'm fine, mother, but please don't fuss. I'm just glad we're all back safe and sound."

Mildred looked in disbelief as she saw an African, one giant person and a smaller rain-coated man. "George, who are all these people?" she asked with an indignant look.

"Steady on ma'am, let's get inside first. We could do with some lunch. See if cook can rustle us up something. There's a good dear, what?"

"Oh, very well, George. Charlotte, you come with me so we can catch up on what has been going on. You don't mind do you Stanley?" she asked, but Stan didn't really want to let go of his beloved wife's hand. Yet he felt a little let down by Charlie, who had to sit, by her father's wishes, in the front seat of his car. Charlie, on seeing Stan's boyish looks, reassured him with a lip-watering kiss. He let go saying, "I love you princess." Mildred filled the air with her charming orders, particularly aimed at his Lordship.

"George, would you take these gentlemen through to the sitting room?"

Charlie's mother was overcome with happiness, knowing her daughter was now safe. Arm in arm, mother and daughter walked down to the kitchens to find Mrs Baxter. She was the cook who had been with the family for many years. She was very glad to see the return of Charlie and gave her a big hug.

"Bunny," asked Charlie using the pet name that she had given to Mrs Baxter as a youngster "what are you doing here? I thought you were at Whitehaven."

"Well my dear, where-ever your mother goes, then I go too."

"Charlotte, dear," Mildred interrupted, "your father

and I will try to explain everything to you. But not now, there are more important things to see to. We have visitors, Mrs Baxter, seven in all. Could you rustle up some lunch for us?"

"Certainly, your Ladyship, how about a nice salmon and chicken salad?"

"I'll leave it entirely up to you, cook, but that does sound very nice, thank you!"

Mildred and Charlie then made their way to the sitting room, talking constantly about Charlie's ordeal. The group of gentlemen were laughing and chatting about different things when the two women came through the door. It went quiet as George stood and introduced them all to Mildred. Once all familiarities had taken place, order came amongst the now quietening group. Discussions soon started to take place.

Jim asked George where the second entrance was to be found.

"What's that? Oh yes, that, entrance. It's down in the basement. Pretty dark place it is too!"

"I would like to go and look at it, if you don't mind. I have to know it's safe."

"Safe?" uttered George, "Of course it's safe, had the workmen brick it up, what!"

"Well, what I actually mean is that no unwanted guests can come through it, or disappear into it. You'll remember George, how the vortex can appear."

"Ah, see what you mean, old chap, see what you mean? I'll take you down now, if you like. Oh, hold on a minute. Excuse me dear, did the cook say when lunch would be ready?"

"I should think within an hour, George."

"Excellent, plenty of time." said Jim, "Theodore, perhaps you would accompany us?"

"Certainly, but I think we should take precautions. I'll just pop out to the car and get our tools."

The tools Theodore brought back with him were, in fact, two silver crosses. Once Theodore came back, George then took the men down to the basement where work had obviously taken place. The atmosphere didn't go unnoticed, however, since the temperature of the dark place was eerily chilly.

"My God," commented Jim, "the place is active! Look at the floor over here. It's almost glowing. Do you see that, George?"

"Good God, man, the floor is almost bright green! This is the area I had bricked up. Are you sure we're safe down here?"

"We will be in a minute," Theodore said as he hurriedly took out one of the crosses and placed it in the centre of the glowing, green area.

The greenness subsided, leaving what looked like just a normal floor.

"I think that we were just in time, gents," said Jim. "When we get a vortex like this, that is turning green, it's usually because either someone or something paranormal in nature is either coming in here or going out, into this void. Since we are the only ones around, I would presume that something is trying to come out. I believe we just made it in time. We were lucky."

"You mean," sputtered George, "that one of those creatures was coming into my Manor? In Dickens' name, who could it have been?"

"I rather think that it was our two friends, Bill and Edna Cartwright." Exclaimed Theodore who, still standing close to the vortex, seemed to be examining the darkened cellar. Wine racks stood proudly against the damp walls with only a single dull bulb hanging from the ceiling, for light. Many wooden boxes were placed in a stack in one dark corner. "If my theory is correct, then they are the instigators of all that has been going on. We have, for the time being, stopped their antics. We can rest in peace, this night. Well then, gents, I suggest that we go back and join the others and perhaps work out our next strategy."

"Yes, let's get out of here," commented George, "it's not a place that I want to linger, and besides, grub should be ready soon!"

CHAPTER 20

The cook had, as usual, surpassed herself in her culinary skills. A spread fit for a king awaited the arrival of its guests. George commented on how the cook could possibly arrange such a beautiful lunch in such a short time. They all agreed and furnished their thanks to a very modest woman.

Charlie made sure the quiet Detective Inspector, Russell Brown, was positioned next to her at the table. It wasn't without purpose though, she knew, and wanted to know more about this seemingly quiet, strange, yet intelligent soul. Her motives were, therefore, to question him on whether it was police business, or a more personal interest.

Soon everyone was tucking into the lunch, wine flowing like it was going out of fashion. Mildred sat by George, giving her poor husband the third degree. Charlie, on the other hand, hardly gave the detective time to breathe. He seemed to be struggling on a major decision: which type of cutlery to use for the various dishes.

"So then," Charlie launched, "Inspector Brown, are you on police business, or what?"

"Oh, sorry, ma'am, er Miss, no, certainly not. I can see where you're coming from though. Yes, it must be very strange for you all."

"Come on, Charlie," insisted Stan, "let the good detective eat in peace!"

"Hmm, no, sir, it's quite all right. I expect it is quite unusual for a police officer, like myself to be involved in such a strange situation. No Sir, Ma'am, my police business finished before I decided to have a few days off."

"Inspector, please call me Charlie. You see, while my mother may like this titled nonsense, I really don't care for it myself. So, what are your motives? Most police officers wouldn't dig this far into a case."

"My apologies, Ma'am, oops, sorry, Charlie. My interests are purely of a personal nature. You see, Charlie, I've always had a bit of an interest in spiritual business, especially after I attended a lecture on mediums. In fact, it was with our very own Mr Hawkins. I was so taken by it I attended even more of his seminars. Very interesting. Yes, very interesting. We have, although I'm not allowed to give details, used Mr Hawkins in a couple of our cases. They produced very good results."

"But how are you going to write this case up, I mean, wouldn't it cause some sort of investigation on its own?" Charlie queried as she picked up her glass of white wine.

"Quite Miss, quite. It does pose a bit of a problem, but this one will be written up as solved. In other words, you could have gone on a holiday, or maybe you visited a sister. You just forgot to tell anyone. You see, Miss, I mean Charlie, who would believe a story about the supernatural? I mean holes that just appear in walls? Creatures, with horns sticking out of their heads? And what about a lost village that exists in time zones? No Miss, I would be the laughing stock of the police force. Maybe now, you can understand why I had a few days holiday from work. It was something I was interested in, something unusual and something a lot more exciting than my otherwise dreary job."

"Well," blushed Charlie, "that certainly shuts me up, doesn't it? Still, I am very thankful you did get involved. You were quite brilliant in that cavern. It looks like you'll have to find some sort of excuse for my Stan, won't you?"

"Thank you, er, Charlie. Yes, we'll have to think about that one, but don't worry, it's just paperwork you know."

"Ladies and gentlemen," intervened Jim, "may I propose a toast to thank our hosts for their generous and most pleasant lunch and, of course, to their very lovely Manor."

They all happily agreed, celebrating with the tingle of their wine-filled glasses.

"Ah, yes," replied George, "as soon as everyone has finished lunch, we'll go into the sitting room. I expect we have a lot to discuss."

George was certainly right about that, for as soon as the group were ready, they filed into the sitting room. The atmosphere seemed a little tense, as quietness finally becalmed the room. Only the chiming of the tall grandfather clock, which stood proudly by one of the picturesque walls, interrupted the quietness.

"We'll begin our debriefing," murmured Jim. "Does anybody have any questions?"

"Yes, I do," piped Jack. "Why do you think those devils didn't die with the silver bullets and arrows?"

"This is a good question," spoke out Theodore, "but not one that I have a good answer for. What we have to remember is that these creatures are not your average animals. They come from a world we don't understand and one we never will. It does seem though, that by placing the crosses on their bodies, we were able to curtail their activities."

"Yes, I would agree with that, Theodore," said Jim, "but it appears that only human or, should I say, reprieved souls from beyond the grave can be brought back to some sort of life by Satan. His followers, though, are very susceptible to any silver, crosses, bullets, arrows, or other types of weapons made from silver. I believe that our friend Jack has a name for these individuals?"

"Dronians, they're called Dronians! These are the ones you describe as followers. The animal creatures, as you call them, are known as Satanicals. My predecessors told these names to me. God bless their souls! They belong to the hierarchy of Satan himself. The Dronians are directly controlled by these Satanicals who use them to do their work for them."

"And what, pray, is their work?" asked George.

"Simple really, to make sacrifices to Satan. It seems that our evil lord of the dark realms has a plan to rule the world, via his followers."

"Hold on there, Jack," Jim begged, "how do you know that this is his plan? What leads you to conclude this?"

"Simple really. It's the increase in the number of

Dronians. Over the years that I have been trapped in that time zone, I have noticed the increase of the Dronians. More and more people are being snatched or, should I say, lured by the Dronians that can masquerade as such people like Stan and Charlie's housekeepers. The Dronians are very good at this. It seems to me , from what I have observed, that they get themselves a job, then make ready for an area within the premises, household or whatever, for a vortex to assert itself."

"If this is true," asked Theodore, "then why don't the people who are snatched rebel when they are within the village?"

"Not much chance of that," Jack warned, "I'm afraid. You see, when an innocent person goes through the vortex, it surprises them. Their inquisitive nature takes them through the cavern. No one or nothing to stop them. They go out into the open countryside, spot the village and continue on to it. Once there, the normal looking villagers, although they're Dronians, greet them. Once they are in that situation, they are hypnotised. They seem quite unaware that this has happened to them and become like the rest of the Dronians. With a bit more work on their minds, they are soon enveloped into the community of the Dronian lifestyle. Rituals are commonplace in the village, so that new Dronians believe they are given immortality, through the Satanicals.

Now then, since the Dronians are of a live human form, silver weapons or crosses, unlike the Satanicals who seem able to overcome most attacks, can conquer them. They have immense strength, as we have already found out. These, my friends, are the ones we have to try to avoid. From what I have seen, I have no doubt that they could easily rip you or anything else, come to that, apart!"

"From what I saw," said Charlie, "I would back Jack up. Those Dronians are more than a match for most of us."

"Eh, what?" gulped George, "It sounds as if it would take an army of men to stop these creatures, eh?"

"Excuse me, Sir," piped up Detective Brown. "Jim, I seem a little confused. You say that Mr and Mrs Cartwright died, many years past, but they were resurrected by the creatures you call Satanicals? Now, what I am concerned with is, if that is indeed the case, and I have no reason to disbelieve any of it, then what sort of percentage would these resurrected souls be within the village? And how many "snatched victims" are we talking about? I ask this because there should be records of these missing people and also, does anyone believe that there may be a difference in physical strength, between one Dronian raised from the dead, compared to one that has been lured into the community?"

"Well, you're very observant, Russell, but I think Jack might be able to answer your questions."

"I've seen no difference in strength between any of the Dronians." Jack continued. As for how many people have been lured into the community altogether, I just don't know. I have not had the privilege of seeing any resurrections, but I have seen about twenty people, including Charlie, come through that devils cavern. That is within the last three months. Russell, I'm pretty sure you want to know why I didn't help those people when they appeared at the cavern's entrance. Would that be right?"

"To tell you the truth, Sir, that would have been my next question. But I rather think you would have a good reason not to help them!"

"You're right about that. The only thing that stopped me, my dear Detective, is that although these people coming out of the cavern thought that they were alone, they were, in fact, being watched by several of the Dronians. I almost fell into the trap one day, when I noticed two people coming out from the entrance. I came out of my place of safety thinking that I could help them, but then I spotted one of these Dronians, hiding amongst the rocks. I quickly backed off into the trees and watched what happened. Thank God I wasn't spotted, because as the two people went towards the village, I saw another three of the devils. They tracked them all the way to the village, keeping themselves out of sight. I hope that satisfies anyone's curiosity."

"Well sir, I mean, Jack, that is exactly what I was thinking. Tell me, Jack, do you think this cavern entrance is regularly guarded?"

"I wouldn't say that it was guarded all the time, but it became clear to me that there seemed to be more activity than there normally was. Before I went anywhere from the safety of my trees, like when I had to go hunting, I would always check the area of the cavern first."

"Do you know, Russell," added Jim, "I think I see where you are coming from. If a raid was planned, then this sort of information would be invaluable to us. Well done, I'm glad you're with us!"

"Thank you sir, but I hope I'm not imposing myself too much, as a detective, but it is hard to ignore my experience in getting all the information that's needed to ascertain the strengths and weaknesses of our foes. I rather think, Mr Hawkins, sorry, I mean, Jim, that you already have some sort of plan in mind?"

"You're very astute, Russell, but let's see if there are any more questions before we go that far."

"Are we under the impression that there could be more villages in the time zone that are under the influence of the Dronians?" asked Stan.

"We can only surmise this by a deeper investigation." replied Jim. "But usually where there's an influence of this scale, it has a good chance of infecting a wider area. I pray, though, that it hasn't gotten that far yet."

"Don't tell me you are actually thinking of going into that place again, surely?" Mildred piped up looking concerned. "But why? We have our daughter back and of course we have Jack back. Isn't that enough?"

"I can understand your fears, Lady Carberry, but I'm afraid," said Jim, "that if we don't, all hell could be let loose on this earth."

"Let me just explain a couple of things," interrupted Theodore, "firstly, we know that a certain couple, namely Mr and Mrs Cartwright, are coming and going between this world and their own. They are using your Manor and the cottage as their main entrances. If we allow this to continue, none of us will be safe. That includes all of your staff as well. Secondly, both Jim and I have noticed a higher rate of paranormal activity throughout the region. We believe that what we have witnessed ourselves, particularly with what happened to Jack and Charlie, is the main cause of it all."

"Our main problem," continued Jim "is the Cartwrights. They have to be stopped, once and for all. The only way to do that, I'm afraid, is to go back into the vortex, find them, then destroy them."

"But why," said Mildred, "have they picked on this place?"

"I believe, although I might be wrong," waded in Jack, "that it is due to the family curse. Old Thomas, who was there before me, thought this was the reason why any of us were brought into their world. It makes sense to me, anyway."

"I don't like it," Mildred answered. "George, couldn't you use your influence at the Ministry? It sounds to me like you will need proper military action or something like that?"

"What, what, well ... I suppose ... well, I daresay ... well, what do you think gentlemen?"

"I suggest that we slow down a little," replied Jim. "Before we know it, we'll have World War Three exploding around us! No, I can understand your fears, Lady Carberry, but I don't envisage having to use such force as the military. Well, certainly not at the present time anyway. It would be more in the interest of the people to keep a lid on the events at this time. Just imagine if the local community got to word of this, it could cause mass panic amongst them. That would be the last thing that any of us would want."

"We have made the vortex, or portal, if that's what you want to call it, safe for the time being, "said Theodore, "so maybe we ought to make some plans for what we need to achieve."

"Well then," said Mildred, "there's no need for Charlie and myself to be involved, it's much too dangerous."

"Not on your Nellie," refuted Charlie. "I'm not going to be left out of this one."

"George?" Mildred retorted. "Tell her, it's far too risky."

"Oh, now listen, Charlotte, don't you think you've been through enough?"

"That's the point, isn't it? I have valuable experience that would only serve to help us all through this. You only need to ask Jack. Isn't that right, Jack?"

"To tell you the truth, I don't like going against family, or even getting in between them, but Charlie is more than capable of looking after herself. She's proved that much with me. If she hadn't been around, I would have been in serious trouble. No Mildred, she would be invaluable. Her knowledge of that world and what goes on there would certainly be an asset to all of us."

"Oh, very well, but George is definitely staying with me! I think I might need a big strong man like him to protect me and the household."

"What, what? Oh, yes, yes, of course, my dear. You can rely on me!" ascertained a bewildered George.

"There, then that's settled." Jim said nervously. "Perhaps we should leave it for tonight now. It will give us all time to think, as well as time for this lovely family to get back together for a while."

"No need for that," said George, "these women will talk all night anyway. I suggest we get some more drinks out. I think that we deserve it, eh?"

"Hear, hear!" rattled Mildred and Charlie together. They all laughed, signalling a relief from the tension. Apart from Jim and Theodore, the rest of them got up from their seats, as if to stretch their legs. Stan and Charlie came together, hugging each other with Mildred smiling at the lovesick couple. George busied himself with gaining the attention of the butler, while Russell, hands behind his back, inspected the large painting of one of the Carberry ancestors that hung on the wall.

Jim and Theodore, heads together, were still a little concerned about the vortex in the basement. It was agreed, therefore, that Theodore would take guard duty by the door leading to the basement for the first three hours, then Jim for the final hours. They put the idea to the Carberry's, who readily agreed the plan.

CHAPTER 21

Detective Inspector Brown was the first person up the next morning. He went straight down to the door of the basement where Jim sat, reading a book he had borrowed from the extensive library in the Manor.

"Good morning, Sir, any problems?"

"Oh no, Russell, apart from a few vibrations."

"Vibrations, Sir?"

"Nothing to worry about, it's what I would expect. The vortex was trying to shift the cross, but it didn't work. Someone or something in the vortex was obviously trying to dislodge the cross from its position by sending waves of vibrations. I kept checking the whereabouts of the cross, but I expect it was too heavy, even for their powers."

"Well, I am glad you were here, Jim. Shall we go up for some breakfast?"

"Sounds good to me Russell, lead the way!"

The household seemed to be coming alive by now. Mrs Baxter was busy cooking a typical English breakfast, while Stan, Charlie and George had just appeared in the dining room. It wasn't long before everybody was present and biting into tasty sausage, mushrooms, bacon, egg and beans. Afterwards, they all, apart from Mildred, assembled in the comfort of the sitting room, waiting for the first question to arise. It came quickly.

"What weapons are we going to take with us?" queried Jack.

"I can only suggest," said Jim, "that we use similar ones to those we used before. Russell, do you have any more silver bullets?"

"None, I'm afraid, but I can soon get hold of some more. I have a very good contact with a specialist friend of mine."

"I have a hand gun," interrupted George. "It's a bit old, I'm afraid, but still works perfectly well. You are welcome to it, if you want it? Perhaps our illustrious Mr Brown could get bullets to match, eh?"

"That's very good of you, George," said Jim. "Thank you, Russell? Could you possibly obtain silver bullets for this gun?"

"Well sir, I might be able to do better than that. If you want more guns, I can certainly lay my hands on maybe two others, with silver bullets."

"That's brilliant! I'm sure that we'd be a force to be reckoned with, having those! Could you start finding out straight away?"

"I'd be honored, Sir. May I use a telephone? I'll let him know that I'm on my way."

"I'll show you where it is, Inspector," replied Charlie. "This way, please."

"We will, of course, gentlemen," reiterated Jim, "all be wearing the silver crosses you still have with you. Does everybody still have theirs?"

164

"I don't," said Stan. "I must have lost it somewhere."

"Okay don't worry Stan," said Jim, "we'll see what we can do. We're going to need a couple of larger ones, though. Theodore, have we any left?"

"Afraid not. The last two were used in the basement. We put one on the floor to cover the entrance and the other on the door to protect the wider area."

"We should have some in the chapel," George said positively. "Haven't been used for some years, still needs some more work on the old place, eh?"

"I would be most interested in looking at your chapel, George," announced Theodore. "Perhaps I could accompany you. What do you say, Jim?"

"Seems like a good idea. I quite enjoy looking around these old manors, that is, if you don't mind, George?"

"What, oh yes, be delighted old chap, be delighted."

"If you are taking guns," added Jack, "then I'm taking a bow. Seems to me, we may need some silent killing. Need a bit of old silver though, you got any you don't like, George?"

"All my silver is old, Jack, antique, you know. Still, better ask the Lady Carberry. Can't stand the stuff, she can't. Hides it away, you know."

"Well, in that case, I'm taking Charlie and Stan with me. I can use them as hostages if she gets mean."

Laughter erupted at this statement, Charlie laughed so much that it caused her pain in the stomach. Even George couldn't but help laugh a little. They then all went their separate ways. Jack did, in fact, easily persuade Mildred to part with a small number of dented silver plates.

The old blacksmith's furnace, in the yard of the Manor, made easier work for the smelting of the silver plates. Stan was rather intrigued by the process of the smelting and decided to lend a hand to Jack. Charlie already knew about the drill for making the molds, busying herself to find the clay needed. This was made somewhat easier for her to recover a small batch, thanks to, 'Bunny' Baxter. She had told them of the blacksmith's furnace, who used it for the shoeing of horses and all types of different things. She also instructed Charlie where she might find the clay, since this was often used in moldings.

In the Manor, Theodore and Jim were getting the grand tour of the small chapel.

"Marvellous, simply marvellous," said Theodore. "Just look at all of the oak panelling and beam work in here. It seems to have a Gothic charm about it."

"Oh yes," agreed George. "It's all been restored to its former glory. It's not completed yet, mind you, but what a damn fine job my workers are making, eh?"

"I'll say so," said Jim, "this bench seating looks like the original thing."

"Lucky there, old chap," grinned George. "Most of this seating is the original. The rest I had made to the exact replications. Some of the beam work was damaged in the bombing, but lucky for me, I have a good source of old English oak on my estates. Most of it was repaired, though. It amazed me how the general structure survived as well as it did."

A beautiful small font, with its patterned, mosaic-marbled plinth, commanded the eyes to be in awe of its beauty. It stood proudly with its square top of mosaic, boasting a silver bowl at the centre. Although it was cold to the touch, its splendour showed its worth. It stood by an oak lectern, which would have given any priest a certain feeling of humility. He would certainly have been proud to stand by this intricately carved desk, to preach his sermon from. A large wooden cross, some six feet in length, had Christ displayed in his last moments. This ornate feature stood at the back of the preacher's desk.

Several illuminated spotlights were well placed to give a centralized beam of light, although some wiring still needed to be concealed, upon this sanctimonious creation. A spiritual ambience filled the whole of the elaborate chapel, which did not go unnoticed by the adoring gentlemen.

"Do you feel what I do, Theodore?" asked Jim.

"You mean the monk that stands by the lectern, or the woman, praying, in the front pews?"

"Yes, seems like they've been here since the incident."

"What, what do you mean, monk? What woman? Damn it, gents, what incident?" roared the astounded George.

"Our apologies," answered Jim. "These people we are talking about are within the fabric of the chapel. In other words, they are the residual energies of past persons. The monk however, haunts this place from some time back, perhaps around 1680. The woman, well, it seems she is more recent in time terms, perhaps from the 1940's. Oh, the poor lady. It looks like she was in the wrong place at the wrong time."

"Yes, "concluded Theodore, "I agree with that.

The poor woman got caught up in the bombing of the mansion. It seems to me that a wooden beam collapsed from the roof, crushing her body. I know this, because I can feel a great pressure across my own chest. She would have died fairly quickly. I get the impression that she was a member of the household, or perhaps a member of the staff."

"By Jove, do you know of her name?" asked George.

"Her name was Mary, Irish descent I believe. Yes, Riley, Mary Riley."

"My God, so she's come back to visit us! She was one of the maids, you know. Found by the workers who were searching for missing people. Unfortunate, yes, very unfortunate. I'll say one thing about Mary Riley, though, she was very religious. She'd use that chapel every day. God bless her soul."

"That would be about right," said Jim, "but the monk, well, he's a bad force. He was certainly evil. Oh, not to the few local parishioners themselves who would have come here for the service, but to the young boys. It looks, from what I am picking up, that he was very abusive ... let's just say that he used them in a despicable manner. Terrible! Still, he got what he deserved. I'll try to explain. You see, when the owner of this Manor found out what he had been up to, word quickly spread. It seems that some of the men folk, probably the locals, beat him up real good, before he got thrown in a small dungeon under the Manor. He was left to die. He didn't last long anyway; he was beaten so viciously. You may have noticed George that things have been moved around in here. In particular, the large Bible you have on the lectern."

"Well, I can't say that I've seen the Bible move myself, you know. But I have heard rumours, mainly by the staff, of things being moved from one place to another, and even completely disappearing altogether. So, you reckon it's this beast of a monk, do you?"

"I'm afraid so, although we can't rule out the maid, Mary."

"Well, in that case, is he any risk to us?" George wondered, almost standing to attention with his hands on his hips. "I mean, is he a part of all these other nasty creatures, the ones that are under that vortex thing?"

"I would say not," confirmed Theodore, "he is still suffering the torment of his wrongdoing, by being grounded here. As for whether he could become involved with the satanic plan, I don't think he could, because he is a God-fearing man."

"I would have to agree with Theodore," said Jim, "but it is a tricky one, that's for sure. Maybe it's best to send him on his way. Don't you think so, Theodore?"

"That's the best solution in my opinion. What do you think, shall we do it now, if you agree, George?"

"Well I might, if I understood what you mean, gents, by 'send him on his way'?"

"Yes, George," added Jim, "we intend to send him to see his maker. He's trapped here by his own guilty conscience. He will have to face his abominable sins. What we do is join hands to form a circle. This gives us more energy in our thought patterns. Using that energy, I will try to contact the monk and tell him what we are going to do. After that, we ask for the angels of mercy to come and collect him. Quite an easy procedure, really.

But the more of us within the circle, the better and stronger the energy."

"I can't say I have ever seen this sort of thing before, but I would like Mildred to see you work, if you don't mind old chap, eh, what?"

"It's your Manor, George. We're only here to help, so please carry on!"

George seemed excited about the prospect of his wife, Mildred, experiencing and witnessing such an event. Jim and Theodore were a bit bemused by his reaction and tried to fathom out his reasoning. Perhaps George's idea was to convince Mildred that an end could be achieved, to get rid these spiritual beings and, even better, the eventual end of the curse that was laid upon the Carberry name. Whatever reason Lord Carberry had, it was, as Jim pointed out, His property.

Twenty minutes later, George returned, followed by Mildred, Stan and Charlie.

"Looks like we've got a party going on here," commented Theodore. "I hope they leave room for our friend, the monk."

"Ay, we've got the spirits, now all we need is the music, ha, ha, ha!" laughed Jim. "Okay everybody," Jim asked, "will there be any more attending?"

"Jack is still working," replied Charlie. "He said to carry on."

The innocent group gathered themselves between the font and the first row of pews. Both Stan and Mildred felt a little concerned as they all quietened down to listen to Jim.

"Okay then. If we could form a circle, then all link

hands. I'm just going to give us some protection first, so please listen carefully." And then he began, "I ask most humbly for our heavenly body to surround us with the veil of protection, each and everyone of us. To protect us from the dark forces of evil. We ask you to only allow the spirit of virtues. Amen." He looked up. "Please folks, continue to link hands. Here we go then!" The circle was now complete with everyone holding hands.

He continued. "If the spirit of the monk is with us, we ask you for a sign of your presence. Make a tapping sound, touch one of us, or show us your energy."

The chapel was very silent as Jim called out. Then, suddenly, a low tapping sound, quite close to the group could be heard. Gasps of nervous people had them looking at each other, as if to check that no one was making these sounds. Quietness soon regained the atmosphere, as Jim continued his inquisition, contact with the spirit confirmed.

"Thank you for joining us. I know your name is Joseph. Why are you still here? Do you fear your God?"

A single, sightless tap indicated the monk understood and agreed with Jim's question. Jim continued to ask if what he had done to the innocent boys caused him resentment of his evil actions, and that he needed help to cross over to the light. Again, a single tap could be heard.

"You will be given the opportunity to redeem yourself with the Lord. Before I send him back, do any of you want to ask him any questions?"

"Yes, I would." said the enquiring voice of George. "I'm sure that my wife, Mildred, would like to see more than just a few taps on the woodwork. Show us if you can move or open the Bible on the desk."

To the surprise of George and particularly Mildred, the Bible suddenly opened and pages were seen to move by themselves. A crashing sound immediately followed this psychic phenomenon. The sound was that of workman's toolbox, its lid had been slammed shut. Mildred fainted at the abrupt sound, falling with a thud to the ground.

"Good Lord!, Mildred!" shouted George in panic.

The circle broke its grasp as Charlie and the quivering Lord of the Manor quickly wafted air around the face of the stricken wife and mother. Mildred soon recovered though, with the help of a glass of water, which was conveniently fetched from a small washroom next to the chapel, thanks to Theodore. She profusely began apologizing to the entire group, as her embarrassment grew.

"Please, I'm alright. I'm so dreadfully sorry, it must be the heat in here. Please continue."

"If you are sure, Ma'am," expressed Jim.

"Heaven knows, yes, I'm fine now."

"In that case, it won't take a minute." Jim restarted his communication. "Everybody please rejoin hands. 'I ask, with a humble mind, for the collection of this poor tormented soul to be taken up by the angels of mercy. Our Heavenly Father, we thank you. Amen.' There, it is done! This man 'Joseph', will now be taken from this place forever."

The group broke the link with a saintly reverence.

CHAPTER 22

Charlie, who had previously linked hands with Theodore, noticed he hadn't let go of her hand. She could feel him trembling slightly, so she asked if he was all right.

"Oh, I'm sorry, Miss Charlie, it always happens to me. I mean, when the angels of mercy come to collect a lost spirit, it feels as though I am part of the rush of wind as they go by, with said spirit in tow. Nothing to worry about. I'm just a little bit more prone, or should I say humbled by the presence of the angels."

"How wonderful," Charlie joyfully said, "you must be highly blessed to feel that close to the spirit world. I wish I was like that. It must be a wonderful feeling."

"Indeed, Miss Charlie, but we are only God's instruments, a channelling tool for people who wish to have direct contact between this world and the spirit world beyond. I am, without doubt, like Jim, extremely privileged to have these gifts. You know, Charlie, even you could have this special bond, provided you have love, faith and feel a need to help people with their desires of being closer to their departed relatives and friends."

"But how can a normal girl, like myself, attain such

gifts? Surely people like you and Jim are born with these special powers?"

"Oh, Miss Charlie, no, everyone has the will if not the mind, to attain the link of spiritualism. Yes, it is true that a few people are gifted from a very early age. If they weren't, it may have slowed things down a little, in how the movement progressed. But the important thing here is that we all choose our own destiny. We are given the choice to decide which path to travel. Destiny is decided by these paths, but when we find the right one, then it is through our own self consciousness. Do you see the sense in that?"

"Well, I've never heard of these paths you speak of, but yes, I suppose we do make up our minds about the way we want to live."

"That's about it. If you feel you would like to learn more about spiritualism, then either myself or perhaps even better, because of locality, Jim, would be only too pleased to show you the way we work. See us when we have completed our task though, because we have much work to do. I'm sure we will talk further about this subject at a later date, okay?"

"Thanks, Theodore, I'll keep you to that."

George escorted Mildred back to the sitting room, where they sat chatting about this new event. With a slight glee, he couldn't help pondering his thoughts to Mildred.

"I told you these gents were good, now do you believe me?"

"Yes, George, I do. I'm not certain about all of it though. I mean, well, I didn't actually see a spirit or something like that, did I?"

"By God, woman, how do you think that big heavy Bible moved all on its own, eh, what?"

Their conversation continued until Mildred was called away. Charlie, on the other hand, wondered if things could be so straightforward, considering her own experiences up to now, even having seen the rather dark side of a different world that portrayed such evilness. Comparing this with her world, which portrayed such tranquillity and love was, to say the least, a little perturbing. She returned back to Jack, who still seemed to be busy with his newfound toy, the furnace.

Jim and Theodore were the last ones out of the small chapel. They found what it was that they were looking for: two silver crosses. These would be invaluable tools of the trade.

The knock at the large wooden front door signified the return of the illustrious, but as usual, apologetic Detective Inspector Russell Brown. He carried a large backpack, which he eagerly placed upon the oak table within the library. The rest of the group, upon hearing Russell had returned, filed into the same room.

"My God," blurted out Stan, "it looks like you've bought enough arsenal to start a war!"

"To tell you the truth sir," the puffing detective answered, "my supplier thought the same."

The group gathered around the table to view the weapons. He produced two standard police issue revolvers, one semi-automatic machine pistol, two boxes of hand-made silver, .45 bullets, each containing one hundred rounds and one box of semi-automatic machine gun bullets, three hundred rounds.

"I'm afraid we'll have to share the silver bullets, gents, but I've got the same calibre as my own revolver. I've brought along the semi, purely as back up. There are no silver bullets for that though, but it may come in useful, just to slow those creatures down a little. Does anybody have any experience with a semi?"

"I do," answered Jim, "used several in the later stages of the war. I'll test it out round the back later. Stan, if you and Theodore want to familiarize yourselves with the revolvers, then we'll do it together. Okay, gents, if everybody is here, we'll sort out a plan of action. How did the bow making go, Jack?"

"Aye, all done. Two bows, one for Charlie and one for myself, complete with silver-tipped arrow heads."

"Ah, that's good." Jim confirmed. "Now then, gents, oh, and Charlie, I'll tell you what I think. Some of you may wonder why we sought out more silver crosses. Well, the way that I see it, if two of the crosses were placed upon the altar, that's the one in the cavern, we should be able to stop the Satanicals rearing their ugly heads above it. That's the theory, anyway. If we do manage to achieve this, then we'll only have the Dronians to worry about. Our main aim is to put an end to our notorious friends, the Cartwrights. They-and both Theodore and myself agree, are the ones responsible for luring innocent people into the vortex, also, in some way that we can't even make a guess about, the vortex itself. We have to take these people out of the equation permanently! I'll make it quite clear, there'll be no prisoners. We expect, and certainly hope, that once we have completed these tasks, then there will be no more Satanicals and no more

Cartwrights that can influence an up-rising. Well, ladies, gents, that's what we have to do and I'm sorry for being so straight to the point. Are there any questions?"

"Suppose," asked Stan, "that the Satanicals are already within the cavern, what then?"

"Then there'll be an almighty fight," replied Jim. "But it appears the Satanicals are only present when there is a sacrifice. I can only presume that theory though, so let's hope my instincts are correct. Let's hope one isn't taking place when we go in. We won't really know until we enter the cavern, but we will be well armed and ready for such an event. Sorry, but that's how it is."

"I think we may be missing one important factor," said Jack, "we may not even end up in the same cavern where we were before!

"I quite agree, but since we have your knowledge of the area, I'm sure we'll find the right place. I'm not saying this is going to be easy. It may go terribly wrong, so let's hope and pray that lady luck is on our side. Jack?" Jim turned towards him putting his large hand on Jims shoulder. "Since you have the best knowledge and experience of the land and the habits of these creatures, it seems you are the obvious choice of leader. Does everyone agree?"

They all nodded their heads in agreement, without hesitation.

"Why don't we just go into the cavern from our cottage?" wondered Charlie who had straddled up to Stan, listening hard at Charlies' way of thinking.

"Simply," replied Theodore, who seemed unable to look directly at Charlie, knowing that the cottage would never again be lived in. "because we don't know what, or who, is lurking there. It would be very dangerous for any of us to enter the cottage any more."

"What do you mean, exactly, any more. That's our cottage, our home!"

Theodore looked at George for support, knowing that he might upset the young mistress even more. Charlie then stared at Theodore, a stare that was full of anger and resentment. Coyly, Theodore looked up at her.

"I'm sorry Charlie, but the future of your cottage could be in great peril. We'll just have to wait and see."

"Quite agree gents, what?" retorted Lord Carberry, moving towards his daughter thinking that she might go too far. "The place has always been a worry to me. Don't you fret about that, Charlie, my girl, it will be all right in the end, eh?"

"Oh papa, I do hope so," she blurted out with a tear in her eyes.

"Charlie," butted in the calming voice of Jim, "it may be worth remembering that lives could be at stake with the cottage, so we'll leave that one to last, okay? Now then, gents, the way I see it, if Theodore and myself go in first, followed by Jack, Russell, Stan and Charlie, then we can assess the situation, depending on where we are, then Jack can take over. Once we find the right cavern, we will place the crosses on the altar and work from there. That seem all right to you, Jack?"

"Yes," agreed Jack, pointing towards Charlie, "but I want Charlie by my side. A bow is much quieter than a gun. We may need the element of surprise, so it will be to our advantage. We'll have to play this one as we go along. So, the question is, when do we go Jim?"

"I estimate," he was scribbling something on a notepad, "that once we have a few essential supplies, a bit of food and water, we can go at about nine o'clock. George, would you be good enough to supply us with what we need?"

"What, oh, yes of course. Mildred, my dear, could you get cook to take care of this, eh?"

"I'll attend to it straightaway," she replied noticing that Jim was holding out a piece of paper for her attention.

"Here's a list of what we'll need Madame." Jim handed the list over to Mildred studying it with a quick glance. Mildred then went out of the room.

"Now then, George," continued Jim, "I'm afraid I have to ask you to do a very important job. That is, to guard our escape route, at all costs. Do you think you could do that for us, Sir? It could be dangerous work, but we need someone we can rely on."

"You chaps need not worry about it. I'll stand on duty like a sentry. Yes, I'll dig out my old army pistol and maybe my sword," George gave the actions of holding a sword high up in the air. "Solid silver, don't you know? Be a pleasure, quite a pleasure. You'll be safe enough with me around!"

"That's great George, thanks. Jim then moved back over to the table where the guns lay. Picking one up, he examined it. "Okay, time to check out these guns. Stan, Russell, are you ready Stan, Theodore?"

CHAPTER 23

The basement was cold, icy cold in fact and this did not go unnoticed. Lord Carberry pondered whether or not to fetch his warmer attire, but then noticed an old coat hanging by the many racks of wine. This he promptly put on and gave a sigh of relief.

"Everybody ready?" said Jim as he removed the cross on the glowing greenish floor, handing it to George for his own protection.

In amazement, the brick floor disintegrated before their very eyes. Jim walked into the area of the vortex, to find himself on a small landing, with a set of brick-built stairs.

"It's okay." He remarked carefully placing his feet. "There's some stairs here, so be careful where you step though, could be a bit slippery."

Charlie was the last person to vanish into the void, amidst the bewildered look of Lord Carberry.

The team entered into a fairly large cavern, although not quite as large as the one they had entered before. Jim produced a powerful torch and carefully checked for unwanted visitors. It was quiet, very quiet in fact.

"It looks deserted," he said. "This certainly isn't the cave we want. Jack, it's time for you to take over."

"I'm with you. First things first, so let's see if we can get a bit more light in here!"

Quickly, scanning around the cavern, he found several old fashioned torches made of wooden handles with heads of flammable material on top. He lit the first one, which he had taken off the wall, then continued to light the rest.

The cave suddenly took on an appearance of death. Skulls could be seen in fashioned inlets in the cavern walls. There were also urns of various shapes and sizes scattered around in various places. Theodore had, by this time, started to look closely at the many different objects that surrounded them.

"This is absolutely fascinating," he said, "some of these symbols go right back to the times of the dark ages. I must examine these further, if we get the chance."

"We aren't here for an archaeological expedition, I'm afraid," Jack commented as he visually scanned the musky damp cave. "Well, not yet, in any case. I've found the entrance over here, so I'm going to take a look. You stay here for a minute. Charlie, you're with me. Just watch my back, okay?"

Charlie gave Stan a quick kiss as she resumed her position next to Jack. The pair soon disappeared through the dark, damp tunnel. The floor was so slippery and damp with moss that great care had to be taken, since a fall could cause injuries. Jack's torch shone the way as they stealthily made their way through the narrow labyrinth of passages. These were confirmed when the passage that they were in came to a small opening where two separate passages were visible.

"Hang on, Charlie, said Jack putting his hand up, "we'll get the rest of the party up here first. It looks like we may have to do a split here. You go back and bring them to this point. Here, take my torch and for Heaven's sake, be careful. I want you back in one piece!"

"Will you be all right, Jack? You'll be in pitch blackness."

"Don't you worry about me, just tell them to be quiet as they come through."

As Charlie disappeared, Jack's eyes scanned the area as if he expected something to jump out at him. But it was extremely quiet. The only sounds he could hear were those of Charlie's footsteps, disappearing down the passage.

Jack wasn't the sort to take too many risks, so he found a small, sandy-colored rock and put a mark, an arrow, on the passage he had come from. This, he thought, would ensure that, in case of emergencies, there would be a clear way back. By following these marks, they could simply be tracked by anybody who needed them.

Jack knew it would take Charlie a few minutes to get back, so, once his eyes had got used to the dark, he decided to make a quick scout of the first of the two passageways. He only got a few yards, then turned back and did the same with the other passageway. He noticed that the moss, in this second tunnel, had the impression of being crushed, as if someone or something had trodden it down flat. He then turned to wait at the entrance for the others to catch up, sitting on a large rock. Within minutes he heard the rest of the group making their way to his position.

"I'm pretty sure," Jack explained to Jim as they arrived, "this passage is the one that we want," he pointed out. "This other tunnel probably leads to the surface."

"How are you sure of that, Jack? Jim queried.

"Well, that one over there has an uphill incline. It also seems to be narrowing the further you go, whereas this passage has been used recently. You can tell that by the crushed moss, see that?" He walked with Jim to show him the crushed moss. "This passage is also slightly on the decline."

"You're very astute, Jack. You don't miss a trick. I think that's why we chose you in the first place, to lead us through unknown territory. Well done! We'll follow your advice."

The team followed silently and very carefully behind Jack. It was slow going, especially for the gentle giant's size, as he had to bend quite low in this very damp and slippery tunnel. After some twenty minutes, Jack halted them abruptly with his hand held high.

"Stand still everyone, douse the torches, quickly."

They all did as Jack ordered, while he silently crept forward, as if he knew something was out there. Maybe it was just his senses or somehow he knew where he was. Within minutes, he re-appeared.

"Jim, we're at the main cavern. I couldn't hear anything so presume the coast is clear. You'll need to go in first, with Theodore."

The pair came forward then stopped to take out the two large silver crosses from the knapsack. Jack and Charlie took up defensive positions, just inside the main cavern, keeping an eye on the entrance to the outside world. All, at this time, seemed to be deserted.

Without showing any fear, the crosses were place upon the large altar. An immense screeching rose up in a luminous green, foul smelling mist. The echo's made Charlie shiver, but it soon ebbed away. Jim couldn't help his surprise reaction of beating the Satanical's in their own dwelling.

"We've done it, Theodore!" he announced triumphantly. "It's okay, Jack, bring the others in."

The stench of death faded as Russell and Stan came through into the main cavern. Stan immediately rushed to Charlie's side.

"Are you alright?" he panicked, "I've never heard anything as piercing as that before. It frightened the life out of me!"

"I'm fine Stan, but just as frightened as you. Look, Jims trying to get your attention."

Jim immediately ordered Stan to run to the main entrance, so that he could act as a lookout. The detective haplessly wandered over to the shimmering altar, standing quite still, as if contemplating the strange scenario that confronted him.

"It is most impressive, is it not Mr Brown?" said Theodore, "an entrance to a vile world."

"Indeed it is, Sir. Tell me, do you think these crosses will keep the creatures trapped?"

"Well, providing nobody ever removes them, then yes, they should keep us all safe from whatever world lies beneath it."

"Hmm, yes, that's what I thought." Said the detective, stroking his chin and seemingly not convinced.

By this time, the other members of the team had

gathered around the altar and were listening to the words of this quite intriguing conversation. Jack stepped forward.

"My God, yes, I can see what you are thinking, Inspector. It seems as if we have forgotten an important issue here. What Russell is thinking, gentlemen, is that if we don't destroy at least the main entrance to this cavern, once we're finished that is, then anyone could walk in here and remove the crosses. We all know what would happen then, don't we?"

The team stood motionlessly then the Inspector spoke once more.

"Indeed, Sir, which is why I brought along something for that possibility."

He took off his rucksack and produced several sticks of dynamite, along with a roll of fuse cord. The group were quite dumfounded by this clever forward thinking genius.

"Well, Russell," added Jim, "it looks as if we are in your debt, once more. Your foresight goes before you. I'm glad you have come along, well done. Now, gents, sorry, and you, Charlie, we have to get to the village. Remember though, our main aim is to take out the Cartwrights, but anyone who gets in our way, we'll take them out also. Jack, we are in your hands again. Okay, first thing. We'll need a volunteer to stay here and guard our way back. The person will also be responsible to keep anyone out of here. So then, do we have a volunteer?"

Silence fell upon the group, until Russell spoke out.

"If I may say, I think I would be best suited for this job. I have experience in dealing with dynamite. Goes back a few years, but it shouldn't be a problem."

"No, I don't agree," insisted Theodore, "you are the best shot with a gun, invaluable for the sort of work that needs to be done. No, I think that I should stay behind."

"I agree with Theodore," interrupted Jack, "it's true that Russell is a great shot with a gun, but Theodore has the experience with the paranormal. It may well be needed in this cavern. I suggest that you, Russell, show Theodore how to set the dynamite. Do you agree?"

Russell accepted the decision and took Theodore to the various points in the cavern where he needed the dynamite to be placed. The team quickly got everything sorted out then, led by Jack, they started towards the village.

Pausing for a brief moment, they looked towards the spinney of upturned trees, where Jack and Charlie had hidden out.

"Good God," Jim said with a surprised look on his face. "I wouldn't have believed it if I hadn't seen it with my own eyes."

"Aye," replied Jack, "take a good look at it. If we get into any trouble and can't get back to the cavern, then that's the place to head for. It was my home for many years, and Charlie's, for a short while. No one will enter the sacred trees, only us, okay? Keep close, everybody, and if I say down, hit the ground without hesitation. Is that clear? We don't have far to go, so let's get moving!"

Jack moved like a professional soldier, eyes constantly searching every nook and cranny. Using the fence lines to their advantage, they kept out of sight of any intruder they might meet. Dirt tracks were the only style of roads that existed in these parts, but at least they offered a slightly easier route towards the village. As they neared, Jack ordered everybody down under the protection of a hawthorn fence structure. Scanning the village, he saw a few people mulling around. It looked like a normal village to anyone who came across it, but this team knew better. They knew also that they would have to kill what appeared to be normal looking human beings. They were, in fact, servants of the devil, who had to be destroyed at all costs. Once Jack had completed his survey, he returned to the group.

"Listen up, people," said Jack gathering the group towards him. "We'll need to go through every cottage to find our friends, the Cartwrights, so I suggest we split into two groups. Russell, you go with Jim to the first cottage on the left, I'll take Charlie and Stan to the other end of the village. We'll go up by the church, but round the back, through the graveyard. We'll then try to take out the ones who are moving about. With any luck, we'll start coming up through the village, house by house. Jim, wait until you see those stragglers keel over, then go into your first objective, then make your way towards the top end. You'll have to be fast, in and out, okay? I suggest you get yourselves into position over there." He pointed to the end cottage where there appeared to be a good hiding place, behind its surrounding wooden fence line.

"Sounds like a decent plan, Jack, but what if they hear the racket and come out into the street?"

"I quite expect that, so you'll just have to use that semi to slow them down while the rest of us take them out. This won't be a picnic, just don't underestimate them. They are evil killers and won't hesitate to break every bone in your back!" He then turned to face Stan and Charlie who were holding hands. "Stan, make sure your gun is loaded, but don't use it until I say. Charlie and myself will use our bows, which will give us time to get into position." Jack had to halt Jim and Russell who were eager to make their way to their hiding place. "Jim, don't go just yet in case any one decides to come the way that we came. Once we're out of sight and you're sure everything looks okay, then go. A couple of minutes to get to the church should do. Stan, Charlie, come on, let's make war!"

Charlie had already gone through the same sort of scenario before, so it was no surprise to hear her giving instructions to Stan, strange as it was. She adopted the phrase, 'keeping low is the name of the game'. Stan just laughed at his wife's adventurous spirit. Keeping low while moving quite fast they soon reached the graveyard, undetected and without any problems. They then crept into the crypt beneath the main church. As expected, Jack checked the building, then brought Stan and Charlie to the entrance of the main doorway outside.

"The church is clear. Stan, stay just behind the doorway until Charlie and me get into position. Right, are you ready Charlie? Keep your head down. We're going to creep along the wall to that corner over there, see it?"

"Okay, yes, I see it, I'll follow you."

The pair crept slowly and carefully through the few gravestones that littered the small area in front of the church. They could see two of the Dronians talking to each other, backs turned to them. Another two-one female with broom in hand, were about fifty yards away on the side of the church. Jack whispered to Charlie.

"We'll go for those two first, opposite us. You take the one on the right and make sure of your target."

The pair rose slowly, took aim and with amazing accuracy fired. The two Dronians fell quietly to the ground. They quickly ducked down and moved position.

"Ready?" said Jack.

Charlie nodded, then, as before, they stood, took aim and fired. Jack's target fell with a groan, but when Charlie let go of her arrow, the woman bent down to pick something up. Her arrow skimmed across the woman's head, embedding itself into the cottage door. The Dronian female screamed, shouting out, "Humans! Humans are here!"

Jack reloaded as she started to move towards her cottage, but Jack was too quick for her as his silver-tipped arrow struck her in the stomach. She fell, clutching the arrow, as if trying to pull it out. A curdled, almost wailing, death-defying scream rocked the whole village, as she died in a curled up heap.

Stan rushed out of his hiding place and fired a shot at one of the Dronians, who had walked out to see what was going on. It took Stan another shot to finally bring him down, but not before the dreaded Satanist ran towards him, shouting the alarm to bring the rest of the village out.

"Stan!" shouted Jack. "Over here, with us, quickly!"

By this time, Charlie and Jack had thrown themselves over the four-foot high wall and were standing by the first cottage doorway with their bows at the ready.

"Stan, get in here, shoot first, ask questions later. Make sure you search all the rooms. I'll follow you in. Charlie, Stay by the door and use your bow to defend us from anyone moving this way. You must keep them away while we're inside!"

Stan burst into the cottage, saw a figure, and immediately shot at it.

Charlie already started to shout loudly, warning that a number of Dronians were coming towards them.

Stan continued his search of the other rooms, while Jack ducked back outside to see Charlie already using her bow to good effect. He joined in, moving towards the next cottage and firing his arrows at the same time, which stopped their advancement.

The roar of a semi-automatic echoed throughout the top end of the village. It wasn't killing the Dronians, but it certainly slowed them down, knocking them to the ground. It gave the others valuable time to search and kill the occupants in the cottages.

Jim was very aware of crossover fire. He made sure that he was in such a position so as not to shoot his own comrades.

"Russell!" shouted Jim above the noise, "I need your help. They're getting too near, half a dozen of them!"

Russell heard Jim's plea for help and responded by bursting out of the cottage door he had first cleared. Without hesitation, he walked stealthily towards the Dronians, firing like a man possessed. The semi went quiet as Russell shot them all in quick succession. His aim was second to none, so, one by one, they all fell.

Aware of a figure behind Jim's back, Russell turned in time to shout out to warn him. "Behind you!"

The huge Dronian lurched for Jim's throat, putting an agonizing, squeezing hold on him. Jim could feel himself losing consciousness as he gasped for breath. This was a surprise to Jim, because he wasn't exactly small himself. With every drop of strength he left, he grabbed the Dronian's head away from the back of his own and gave a mighty yank. By bending his body at the same time, he forced his pursuer over his own shoulders. Russell moved in, fast as lightning, waited until Jim had cleared away, then shot the Dronian straight through his temple. The creature died instantly in a pool of blood.

Sitting on the ground, holding his throat, Jim coughed for air as blood dripped down his face. The now deceased creature had, in one last effort, attempted to tear at Jim's face.

"Are you all right, Sir?" asked the out of breath detective peering down at Jim.

"Aye, thanks to you, Russell!"

CHAPTER 24

"Charlie!" yelled Jack. "Stay close to Stan, cover him, but watch out for Jim and Russell! I'm going round the back in case anyone tries to escape. If you spot the Cartwrights, then yell for all you're worth!"

Bodies were strewn all over the village road. Even more were being slaughtered at close quarters at an alarming rate. Jack disappeared with Stan through the next cottage. He was soon around the back of the village, scanning the whole area. It seemed that no one had attempted to escape this way.

Charlie's yell was heard clearly by the fighting force of both men. Jim and Jack rushed to her aid. She fought like a mad dog, knife in hand, stabbing repeatedly at a tall female Dronian. The knife had little effect, only serving to slow this creature down a little. Jim though, had already seen what was happening and had run over to assist Charlie. He had waded in without hesitation, grabbing the mad Dronian from her back. Trapping her flailing arms, he lifted her completely off the ground. Lifting her high into the air and with such force and ferocity, he slammed her to the ground. Jack took advantage of Jim's work, n made his mark by raising his bow and shooting her with an arrow that penetrated the Dronian's right eye. Death was instantaneous.

"Good God, Charlie," said an annoyed Jack taking her by the arm, "you have to realize, once you stab them with a knife, you must leave it in! They won't die if you don't! Are you all right?"

Charlie's head was bowed down in disgust at herself, as Stan, seeing that she was alright, continued his onslaught into the next cottage.

"Just a few scratches," Charlie whispered, but it was only because I was sure I saw Edna Cartwright! The Dronian took me by surprise coming from behind me, but it won't happen again, that's for sure."

"Cartwright you say?" Jack's eyes lit up. "Where did you see her?"

"There, over in that window!" Charlie pointed to the cottage opposite. "She pulled back the shutter, I'm sure it was her!"

"Russell is in the next cottage," Jim said, quickly moving towards Russell's location. "I'll fetch him!"

Jack told Charlie to stay with Stan in order to back him up. He then ran over to the cottage, waiting for the sweat-drenched detective, and then both burst in. A door slammed shut at the back of the building as the fleeing woman tried desperately to escape.

Russell pulled open the door, saw her and fired a shot.

She fell forwards, but she was still alive, attempting to crawl away.

Russell drew nearer to the stricken woman then finished her off with another bullet to the skull. Her brains burst out of the front part of her skull, demonstrating the force of the bullet.

Jack came up to where Russell was standing, looking down at the corpse. "You made a mess of her, didn't you!"

"I'm rather afraid I did. I only winged her the first time."" Russell apologetically answered.

"Where's her husband? Any sign of him?" Jack asked.

"I believe that figure over there, in the next field, could be him," assumed Jim who had just come from the cottage after checking it out. He had stood some ten feet away, his hands were over his eyes as a shield from the sun's glare, pointing in the direction of a person running.

"I think you could be right Jim." said Jack, "Could you replace Charlie for a while? We have to confirm whether this is Mrs Cartwright or not? Charlie will be able to tell us. "

Jim obeyed without question as he hurried to fetch Charlie, while Russell followed him out. Charlie soon appeared at Jacks side who warned her that it wasn't a very pleasant sight.

"It's her all right, no doubt." She turned away from the grizzly sight, bending down with a feeling of sickness. "Oh, what a horrible mess. Have you found Bill yet? I bet he's not far away."

"Looks like he got away," Jack answered. "He couldn't have thought much of his wife. He left her here to suffer the consequences. Nope, he's done a runner. Looks like he's gone the same way we came from. We'll get him though."

"You don't mean..."

"Aye, he's headed for the cavern! Let's hope that Theodore is vigilant."

"Shouldn't we get after him?" replied Charlie as they both went back through the cottage.

"Yes, we will. But we need to finish off here first, or they'll be after us. Come on let's finish the job!"

It didn't take long for the last few Dronians to be dealt with. They were very lucky to take them by surprise as they did. The fury of the guns had by now fallen quiet. Just the sound of wild birds could be heard, singing their daily chorus. The team gathered in the middle of the road, regaining their breath, Their thoughts turned to what they had just done, as they viewed the scene of carnage and utter destruction. Jack, the only one not to sit down, pointed out that they needed to move out. .

"All right, people, time to get going. Theodore could be in trouble. Fast as you can gents pleas!"

"I don't know where you get the energy from Jack," Insisted Charlie, looking around the blood stained road. "What about the bodies, shall we bury them?"

Jack laughed vigorously. "Bodies? Take a good look at them girl. Can't you see what is happening to them? You still don't get it, do you?"

Charlie walked closer to where one lay. A horrified squeal erupted from her mouth. The body in front of her was actually dissolving before her very eyes. It was as if somebody had poured acid all over them. A white scum seemed to be bubbling over their entire body. Within minutes, just a fine powder lay on the ground. The breeze took care of the rest.

Charlie searched for where the other bodies lay, but they were gone too. Just dust, blowing away in the wind.

Stan walked up to Charlie, comforting her.

"They're not human my love, not like us."

Jack took full advantage of this phenomenon by hurrying around the road, collecting all of the arrows.

"We may need them again, better safe than sorry!" he announced.

The team started out, but only a steady trot could be managed by the worn out vigilantes. The Satanist destroyers seemed to take an age for them to get within view of the cavern entrance. Once there, an eerie silence finally met them as they entered. There was no sign of Theodore. As they looked around, noticing that the charges were still set, ready for activation, they wondered where he could possibly be.

"Where the hell is he?" Jim asked. "Charlie, check the crosses on the altar!" She crossed the cavern treading carefully.

"Good question," replied Jack looking around for any signs, "he must be here somewhere."

"I think," exclaimed the thoughtful Detective, "that if, let's say, this Bill Cartwright has somehow got into the cavern entrance, a struggle may have occurred, and he got away from Theodore. If this is the case, then we should assume that Theodore has gone after him."

"How the heck could you come to that conclusion?" stormed Stan, edging his way towards Charlie as means of protecting her if anything was to happen. Stan's thoughts were once again, all about the protection of Charlie, remembering his past.

"Well sir, there's blood on the floor, down here and if I'm not mistaken, that looks like Theodore's knife. It looks like there's blood stains on it!"

The group looked in the direction Russell was pointing at. His observations seemed to justify the facts. Theodore's knife was trapped in the edge of a large boulder, easily missed by most, unless they were trained to the standards of a great detective, such as Russell Brown.

"My word, Russell," said Jim retrieving the knife, "you must have eyes in the back of your head, amazing!"

"The crosses are still here," shouted Charlie. "Oh my God, quick, come over here. There's blood stains! They're leading this way!" Stan had reached her by this time amazed to see so much blood. He looked at Charlie, who had clasped her hands over her mouth, reassuring her.

She and Stan stood by the tunnel through which they had entered the cavern when they first came through it.

"Right," Jim said, "listen up everybody. Let's think ahead. First, we try to find Theodore. I think that since Jack is familiar with these tunnels, he should lead with someone of his choice. Second, I believe that if Bill Cartwright does manage to slip us, then we need to be ready for him."

"What do you expect him to do then, Jim?" asked Jack.

"Well, I'm not exactly sure what his plan is, but this place, particularly the altar, would have to be his main aim. If he succeeds in getting to this altar and removing the crosses, then we've achieved nothing."

"Excuse me, Sir, but if I were him," butted in Russell, "then I think I would try to escape the way we came in.

I would expect him to overpower Lord Carberry. Sorry Miss, but I don't think your father would prove to be too much of a match for him. Remember Miss, these creatures can't be killed by ordinary means. They're much too powerful I'm afraid. Anyway, if it was me, I would make for your cottage, Miss. If he has the power to open the vortex, he could be in there before we knew it. With that in mind gents, he would also expect us to follow him. The way that I see it is that he would simply return here and remove the cross's."

"Russell?" pronounced Jim, "I think you are absolutely right! Jack, who do you want with you?"

"Best if I had someone with a gun. Stan, you'll do fine. I reckon you may need Russell for the explosives."

"Okay, Jack. The rest of us will stay here until we hear from you."

As Jack and Stan disappeared into the tunnel, the rest of the team organized themselves within the cavern. Russell stood guard by the main entrance. Charlie stood close to the wall where the vortex was usually formed, and Jim was by the altar, to safeguard any removal of the crosses.

Charlie reported that the semi-circle of silver crosses, that were positioned the last time they were there, had been thrown to one side. Jim told her to re-position them, into a circle, close to the wall. He continued to say that if anything other than a God-fearing human being came into the circle from the opposite side, then they would certainly die. It was a good measure to stop Bill Cartwright from doubling back.

They each took out their supplies, consisting of a drink

and sandwiches. Russell took a good look outside before he attempted to satisfy his thirst and hunger. Strolling back in, he stared up at the ceiling, contemplating the luminous effect of the reddened roof.

"Tell me, Mr Hawkins," he asked, "why does the ceiling glow red like that? After all, the reflection of the floor is a different colour."

"That's a good question, Russell, but I can only surmise that it is because of what is beneath our feet. Red is representative of the devil. I suppose you could say that it is the symbol of human blood, which is given up to resurrect Satan himself. We humans often use this color to represent danger."

"Do you know, Sir, that is one of the best descriptions anyone could have given to me. And do you know, Sir, I would have to agree with you."

"Nice answer that was, Jim," intervened Charlie. "So what about silver? Why does silver, in particular, manage to kill off these dreaded creatures?"

"Purity my girl, purity! Silver is considered as holy. Some believe that the 'Holy Grail' was made with pure silver. Maybe it was, but I wasn't around in those days." He laughed at his own joke, then continued. "Anyway, it certainly works against these devil people, Dronians, Satanicals, whatever you want to call them."

He was just about to take a bite of his sandwich, when Charlie, looking a little smug, said, "Well, what about gold? That's more expensive than silver and most people love to have it."

"Good grief, Charlie," he almost choked, as he bit into the sandwich. "What's this? Question time? Okay, with gold, it is-and this is my own opinion, man's pure greed that makes gold so expensive. 'Pagans' or 'idolisers' would worship just about anything. They have no true God, but many objects, such as trees, water, minerals and the earth and the celestial kingdom are part of these rituals. Just as gold is used to adorn houses and our bodies. Many golden objects though, were used because their owners viewed them as the most precious gift they could give to their gods, since it was expensive and precious to them. But the ultimate sacrifice, as they believed, was always the human one. The only trouble is they were actually feeding off Satan. He was always the winner because he got their souls. Think of it logically, Charlie, how many men have lost their lives for the possession of gold? A heck of a lot more than from silver."

"Fair enough then, Jack." Charlie admitted defeat, tucking into her sandwiches.

"Hmm..." agreed Russell, "yes, a very interesting topic, very interesting indeed."

A few minutes later, while the threesome were quietly enjoying their first meal, Jim suddenly rose to his feet, waving his arms to attract the attention of the others.

"Hold it everyone!" he interrupted, "I can hear noises coming from the tunnel!"

Charlie repositioned herself closer to the altar, as Russell skipped towards the tunnel, revolver in his hand. He had already raised his gun in the same direction of the noises.

"Its okay," Russell reported, "it's Jim and Stan with Theodore."

Out of the tunnel came the two men, holding up

Theodore. Blood was staining his trousers from a thigh injury. His face was also covered with blood from a second wound.

"What on earth happened?" asked Charlie, as she quickly started to dress Theodore's wounds, once Stan and Jack had put him down on the floor.

"Oh, my own fault really," Theodore began. "I was just finishing off with laying the charges, when all of a sudden this mad man stabbed me in my thigh with a knife. He had taken me by surprise, but I managed to get my own knife out and lunged at him, but he kicked it out of my hand before I could inflict much damage. He was so fast, I couldn't believe it! The next thing I knew, he ran towards the altar. I got my gun out and fired a shot at him but I think I missed. I ran at him firing. He managed to move one of the crosses off the altar before running into the tunnel. I stopped to put the cross back on the altar and ran after him. He was very fast, gone without a trace and then I seem to remember slipping on the wet surface then these two gents were talking to me. I must have banged my head as I fell."

"You're very lucky," said Jack, "you were out cold. You're going to have to take it easy. You've got a bit of a concussion." Jack took a sip of water, offered to him by Russell, then looked anxiously towards Jim. "We can't afford to hang about here. We've got to get moving if we're going to stop Cartwright from vanishing!"

"I agree, I think he will try to double back by going to the cottage and open the vortex."

"Pity we can't open the vortex ourselves, from this end," remarked Stan pointing towards where the silver cross's lay, "then we could meet him inside the cottage."

"Well we can't do that, pity though," replied Jim. "So I reckon we'll just have to catch him up. I suggest Jack, Charlie and myself move out, while you, Russell, blow up the entrance and together with Stan, bring Theodore out.

"No problem, Sir, "insisted Russell, "as soon as Charlie has finished with Theodore, we'll set to work."

Charlie finished her bandaging as well as she could. With the help of Jim and Stan, they managed to get Theodore into the tunnel. They lay him down in a safe place, several yards inside, to avoid him being caught up from the ensuing blast. Led by Jack, Jim and Charlie trotted off, with a burning torch to light their way through the maze of passageways.

To make it easier for Stan and Russell to find their way back, Jack said that he would put up extra markings on the walls of the passageways for them to follow.

The shrewd inspector busied himself with making sure the dynamite was positioned correctly. He measured the ignition fuse and set it to a two-minute burn.

"Have you got a torch?" he asked Stan.

"Ready and burning. Here take it, I'll keep an eye on Theodore."

"Okay then, I'm lighting the fuse."

They didn't hurry too much as they entered into the dark tunnel. There, once Stan got close to Theodore, Russell checked his watch.

"Cover your ears!" he announced as time ticked by. "It's going to blow!"

The explosion came with a shuddering blast of flying rocks and a strange howling wind. It rang so loudly that it tore through the tunnel entrance and nearly blew out the burning torch Stan was now holding. The noise echoed through the whole of the cavern system. After the blast, the dust settled down a little. Russell re-entered the cavern, to check its effect.

Grisly howling could be heard dying away from the altar, or where it had once stood. The entombing of the silver crosses, which were now under a huge boulder, quietened this evil sound. The ceiling had collapsed in a spectacular way, destroying most of the cavern, entombing it from floor to ceiling with hard, dense rock.

With a smile, Russell giggled a little, as he thought, 'Oops, must have used too much of explosives!'

He joined Stan and Theodore, who were dusting themselves down. Stan happened to stare up at the ceiling and shrieked with terror as it started to crumble away.

"Good grief, quick, we've got to get out of here! The ceiling is going!"

They picked up Theodore, put his arms around their shoulders and hurried away, going as fast as they could go, as the familiar sound of rocks falling erupted behind them. It stopped almost as soon as it began.

"Well," said Russell as he turned to gaze back down the way they had just come, "I don't think anyone will be following us from that direction."

Jack, Jim and Charlie had by now reached the stairway to the manor basement. They wasted no time in their ascent as they finally came out. It seemed to be no major surprise to them to find his Lordship sprawled out on the floor. They soon realized he must have been attacked by the fleeing Dronian. Charlie wasted no time in getting to her fathers side, fussing over him.

"I'm fine," he declared. "The scoundrel disappeared upstairs. Don't waste time with me, get after the blighter!"

Charlie saw that he had a cut across his head and quickly found out her clean handkerchief.

"Stay with him, Charlie," Jim said anxiously, "we'll get after him!"

Jack happened to turn around from where they had just come. "Good grief," he rattled, "the vortex is dissipating! Charlie quick, stand on the second step, hurry, we have to prevent it from closing!"

She did as she was told, standing on the second step, just under the waning vortex. A sigh of relief came over Jim's face, as it settled back down.

"I'm afraid you'll have to stay there until the others catch up. If you move out of the vortex, our chaps will never get out. While you are there, the vortex cannot close down. It all has to do with time dimensions. I don't have time to explain, just stay in between both this world and the one that we've just come from. Do you understand that, Charlie? You can help our chaps get out first, then it will be fine for you to come out."

"Okay," she protested, "just get that son of a bitch!"

"Charlotte! Oh dear me," the battle-torn lord roared, "language, please!"

"Sorry, Papa." She grinned back.

Once Jim was satisfied that all was well with the vortex and George, they hurried off in pursuit of Bill Cartwright.

The Manor seemed to have come alive with servants rushing around, not quite sure what was going on.

Confusion unsettled the whole of the residency, including Lady Carberry, who, by now, began descending the stairs of the basement. She was followed by two of her house staff.

"That evil person has left the Manor!" she told Jim and Jack as they raced past. "Are George and Charlotte all right?"

"Yes, you'll find them both down there, sorry, can't stop," Jim quickly said.

Jim's car wasn't the fastest car going, but they made good headway towards the cottage. They pulled up to see the door had been smashed through. With caution, they entered the darkened room, only to be confronted by the very man they were after. He was trapped like a mouse in a snare. He had nowhere to go, fearing the silver crosses that were laid by the wall.

With an evil growl and his sharp teeth showing, the vile creature slammed into Jim.

"I'll shoot him," beckoned Jack, "hold him still!"

"No!" Jim shouted, as he tried to stay away from the vicious, snarling jaws. "Get the crosses and lay them into a circle. It's the only way."

With a frantic rush, Jack quickly dispersed the crosses into a rough circle. Jim was mauled badly by the amazing strength of the creature, but managed to force himself and his opponent, with an almighty grip, into the circle.

The power of the once human being disappeared suddenly. Jack released his grip on him and dropped him onto the floor, realizing the effect the crosses were having. He crossed back over from the circle, which now entombed its victim. Wailing like a mad animal, an eerie mist started to envelop the Dronian, growing denser in its strange greenness.

As Jack and Jim watched, a final outburst came from the vaporising mist.

"We will return!" he snarled for the last time, as the mist vanished, leaving just a small mound of ash in the middle of the circle.

The screech of tyres burned to a halt, as Lord Carberry, Stan, Charlie and Russell got out of the car. They burst in, not quite knowing what to expect.

"It's okay everyone," Jim quickly said, "he won't be bothering anybody anymore."

"No, and I'll make sure of that!" ruled his Lordship as he pointed to Stan and Russell, "Stan, Mr Brown, you know what to do."

They nodded in agreement and went outside to the large Rolls Royce they had arrived in. From the boot of the car, Stan produced a large bundle of dynamite and gave it to the Inspector. Charlie raced over to see what the men were doing. She gasped in horror.

"What the hell are you doing with that?" she shouted.

"I'm sorry, Charlotte," answered her father who had followed her, along with Jack and Jim. He put his arm around her shoulders in an attempt to comfort her, "it's the only way to put an end to this evil."

"You mean you're going to blow up my cottage?" Her eyes were full of tears, pleading for the place she called home. "Papa no, you can't, please!"

Jim stepped in quickly, to ease any tension between the two of them. Stan felt sorry for Charlie as he stood silently watching the nightmare unfold in front of her very eyes. He bowed his head in anxiety but his own feelings were that of elation. "Maybe now,", he thought, "this will finally end my own nightmare."

"We're sorry about this, Charlie," continued Jim picking up her hands, "but unfortunately, this is the only way. You see, the remains of this evil are trapped under the cottage. You would never be safe while this cottage remains. To make absolutely sure we have to destroy the entire thing."

"Don't worry about this place, my dear," quoted her father, "your new home is the Manor. You'll live there as lady of the house. Your mother and I were always going to give you the Manor as your inheritance. Trust us on this one, my dear, we'll talk later." His lordships intentions included the destruction of the cottage, from when he first heard the news that his own daughter had been involved in the dreaded curse. He knew that he would have to put a final end to the cottage and thus he had ordered the explosives. It had been kept a secret from Charlie by all the men folk because they knew she wouldn't be very happy with it's destruction.

Tears now ran down her cheeks as Lord Carberry pulled her to him in a fatherly way. He nodded a signal to Russell and Stan to continue with their preparations.

"It's just bricks and mortar, my dear, bricks and mortar." George gently combed her hair, soothing her sufficiently.

Russell and Stan placed the explosives carefully. He set a long fuse, trailing it out of the front door. Stan retrieved some personal belongings, both his and Charlie's, taking them to the boot of the Rolls. It was all set for the cottage's last appearance on this earth. Stan took over from George, hugging Charlie's quivering body.

"Let's clear the area!" bellowed Jim.

The group started to move away from the cottage. Charlie seemed a little better now that Stan was with her. They walked, hand in hand, quietly away. The whole village buzzed with anticipation as more and more of the villagers came to see what was happening. The authoritative voice though, of his Lordship, ordered everyone to keep a safe distance at the far side of the village. A check was made of all the properties and their gardens, for any other inhabitants. When all were accounted for and George was satisfied that everything was being done to ensure the safety of the villagers, he waved his arm to Russell, which was the signal to light the fuse.

Russell calmly took a box of match's from his pocket, then lit the fuse. There didn't seem to be any hurrying from this man as he glanced once more at the cottage. He looked pleased with himself as he strolled back towards the villagers, checking his watch as he went. Five minutes later, the village shook violently as the explosion came. Dust and debris were thrown around. The sound of glass splintering and cracking, sent some of the villagers into panic, cowering behind their neighbours for protection. Although the blast was in a controlled manner, it still made an awful mess. Cheers of laughter erupted from the villagers filled the air, while clapping exploded furiously. It felt like a real occasion for these people, indeed it seemed as though a great party had started. Charlie sobbed once more as Stan stood with her, cuddling and caressing her.

He announced to her that, "It's all over now princess, we can get on with our lives again!"

"Well then," George announced, "that's the end of that, gentlemen. You'll all come back to the Manor, won't you? I'm deeply in your debt."

They all readily agreed. Then George turned towards the villagers and put both arms up to quieten them down. He spoke loudly, inviting them all to come and have drinks at the Manor. More cheers went up from what seemed a delighted crowd, then he spoke again.

"I don't want any of you to worry about the mess I have caused. I have workers coming, even at this very moment, to put right any damage to your properties. They will also clear away the mess of the old cottage. My friends, you all probably know about the curse that has hung over my family for many centuries. With Gods will my friends, I believe that this is now all over. My daughter is safe and we can, I hope, continue our special relationship as landlord and tenants. This village will be the envy of all villages, my daughter will see to that." Shouts of agreement were heard and more applause continued. ,"

It seemed like his Lordship had quickly organized a party. While they all cheered him on, singing "For He's a Jolly Good Fellow", a fleet of trucks arrived. Workers of all description filed out of them, assessing the damage. Carpenters, glaziers and manual workers soon got busy putting the village to rights. The villagers were all taken up to the Manor by a fleet of taxis, that were ordered by George himself. They were soon shown into the great hall, where many had never ventured. Servants quickly started giving out glass's of champagne, directed by the ever faithful butler, James. He seemed to take it in with great ease, considering it happened with little notice.

Theodore was reunited with his friend, Jim, not long after he had returned from seeing a doctor. He had several stitches in his leg, while his head boasted a bandage that covered his wound.

After the villagers had left, George took his guests to the sitting room. His Lordship stood to attention and asked for silence.

"My very good friends, I want you to know how much I appreciate your valuable work. I would like to present you, Russell, Jim and Theodore, with something to show that appreciation."

He pulled three envelopes from out of his pocket.

"This is for you, Mr Hawkins." He handed Jim a cheque for £5000. Then he gave the same to Theodore and finally one for the brilliant inspector.

They all tried to refuse the money, but George Carberry was master of his house and wouldn't take no for an answer.

"If you find it hard to accept this small token of my gratitude," he persuaded, "then use it to fund your investigations of this evilness that has been bestowed upon us. Russell, my dear Inspector, use it to write a book, buy a new car or anything you can use it for. Failing that, my friend, well, donate it to a charity, or even the police benevolent fund. I'm sure that you will put it to good use. Heaven knows, I've give enough to them already" He laughed," so please, for your wife if nothing better, eh, what?"

The hero detective just stared for a moment, speechless, not knowing what to do.

"Well sir!" he finally answered, "goodness me, I believe you might say I'm flabbergasted!" The whole room erupted into laughter, "I've never seen so much money in all my life. Oh, dearie me!" Charlie walked over and landed him a kiss on his forehead, smiling intensively.

"I think, your lordship," said Jim, "that both Theodore and myself shall put this money to good use. We shall use it to further our research into the satanic cult that has decided to rear its ugly head. We may even be able to set up a proper office or a small church where we can hold our meetings and do a service to the general public. This will be by way of us working as mediums. Thank you."

"Hold on there one moment, my man." Quickly confirmed George, "I think we might be able to help out there. I'll come back to that in a minute. Mildred, Ma'am, have you got what we discussed?"

"Of course I have, dear."

"Good, jolly good. Stanley, Charlotte, would you please come here?"

The young couple looked at each other in surprise but rose from their seats and came face to face with the smiling parents.

"Now then," began George, smiling sweetly at Charlotte, who hung on to Stan for dear life. "I promised you earlier that you would inherit this Manor as your right of parentage. Now, normally, this would be upon the death of your Mother and I. But, since we have already got another Manor, 'Whitehaven', it is pointless trying to live in both. We will, of course, spend our days in 'Whitehaven'. This place and, of course, the lands that belong to it, will now be in your names. Thank you, Mildred."

Mildred passed over a bundle of documents, retrieved from the small coffee table. A blue ribbon, with a hand made silk flower on top, covered the heavy bundle. Stan's eyes nearly popped out in disbelief tightening his grip on Charlie, who had her hand over her mouth.

"These documents are for you two. They contain the deeds of this property, along with the lands and rights. Oh, we've included the village, by the way. All of the village properties belong to us, so I have arranged that they will now be under your control. You, Charlotte, will now be known as Lady Charlotte Harrow. The details need not worry you, whatsoever. You will, however, have to sign documents to make it legal and safeguard yourselves and your future family. My legal team are in the drawing room at this very moment, when you are ready for discussions. Well, what do you say, eh, what?"

The room fell to a deathly silence. Charlotte's jaw was wide open. Tears of joy ran relentlessly down her warm, reddened cheeks. She threw herself at her father, almost strangling the life out of him. Stan was almost doing the same to Mildred, kissing her on her cheeks like a man possessed.

"Oh Papa, Mama, I love you so much," she cried.

After the loving, kissing and exchange of affection finally ceased, the seated men arose to give their congratulations within this wondrous atmosphere. Charlie happened to kiss Jack on his face, when to her surprise, she noticed something different about him.

"Jack? Oh my God Jack, what is happening to you?"

"What do you mean, Charlie, I feel fine!" She filled with horror, putting her hands on both sides of her cheeks.

"It's your face Jack, oh God, you've aged!"

They were all surprised by this outburst, and stared intensely at Jack's face.

"I'm sorry, Jack," said Jim, "but you are in an aging process. You'll probably age to that of what you would be normally. What year were you born?"

"Crikey, it feels as if I've been alive for a hundred years! I was born in 1890. What year did you say it was, Charlie?"

"It's 1975, Jack, which makes you eighty five years old."

"Aye, it does at that. Jim, do you think this aging process will harm my body?"

"I suppose it depends on how fast the process works. The best thing I can suggest at this moment is for you to go to the doctors. How you'll explain it to him, heaven knows, but I'll come with you."

"You'll go nowhere my lad," exclaimed George walking towards him, "I have a perfectly good doctor at my disposal. I'll send for him straightaway."

"Thanks, George, that's good of you, er, brother." George scratched his head realising that indeed, he was his long lost elder brother." Meanwhile dear brother, I don't want to be the party pooper. Someone get me some champagne and, for heaven's sake, all of you stop worrying and staring at me!"

"Well," said Stan lovingly holding both hands of

Charlie, "in that case, I think we have people waiting for us, don't we, Lady Charlotte Harrow?"

The party continued as Stan and Charlie went to meet the legal team, anxiously waiting in the library. When they re-emerged, an hour later, Charlie asked her father for a private chat. This he did, willingly. Within another few minutes they called the group to sit down. George returned to his standing position, ready to give a final speech.

"My friends, Charlotte keeps telling me off for calling her that, but I'm sure she will forgive me. Now then, gents, I will continue where I left off. Mr Hawkins, you mentioned something about needing a place for your research and meetings. I believe that, with Charlie, she has agreed to help you out. She has said you may use the chapel for your meetings and anything else, as well as providing you with an office of your own. Mr Philips will, of course, be included in this deal. There is, of course, one proviso gents… "

"Proviso, Sir?" asked Jim.

"Oh, I'm afraid that's where I come in." said Charlie. "You see, Jim, I have an interest in learning the art of becoming a medium. I would also like to help you in your research, if you have no objections?"

"Objections? Of course not, I would think that you will make a great researcher and I would be delighted to teach you about being a medium. But I can't accept your offer. It's far too much for you to give us this home of yours for our work, it's too intrusive!"

"Don't talk nonsense Jim, this is a very big place. We wouldn't even know you were here. Besides, if anything was to happen from those tunnels below us, you would be on hand to deal with it. My lovely Mama, Papa and Stan all agree that this is the ideal place for your work. So, I don't see how you could refuse!"

"Well, I'm not sure, what do you think, Theodore?"

"It is true, Jim, what Charlie says about the tunnels- we could never be absolutely sure. On that basis alone, it is without doubt a wonderful proposition."

"Well, in that case, what can I say, Lady Charlotte? Yes, thank you, we accept your extremely generous… erm… deal!"

"Marvellous, simply marvellous," cheered George. "Of course, it goes without saying, that Mildred and I shall attend your first meeting. I do believe you could have, what do they say, 'a full house'?"

Cheers of laughter erupted as Jim and Theodore went around shaking hands and being congratulated. When it came to Russell though, he looked amused as he stood there, shaking Jim's hand vigorously.

"Sir, may I congratulate you on acquiring such a distinguished location for your work! I wonder, Sir, if you didn't mind, whether I could come along and perhaps bring some colleagues of mine to your meetings?"

"My dear Inspector, I would think that it would be my honour to have you present. The way you have conducted yourself was outstanding. In fact, Russell, I will make you an honorary member for services rendered. I would also be delighted to have you bring along your colleagues. I wonder though, why you would do that. I didn't think that they were the sort to be interested in the spiritual world?"

"Thank you, Sir, but I didn't think I did anything special. As for my colleagues, yes, I think you already know the answer to that one, if I'm not mistaken?"

"Ha, ha, aye, you have me to rights Russell. It looks like you have this uncanny intuition into what people are thinking. It's rather unique you know, perhaps you have the sort of gift that would enhance our cause. Think about it, would you? Now then, about your insight. You're quite right, Inspector, I would love to have your colleagues attend our meetings. The way I see it, is that as mediums, we could offer our services to assist in their cases. This would certainly compliment our stature as 'useful tools' in the advancement of mankind and our cause as spiritualists."

"Indeed, Sir, although you do seem to lose me with your words. I must admit though, I first got the idea from a TV programme where mediums were used to help solve a murder case in America. I can only see this sort of venture as very promising."

Just then, Jack walked back into the room, after seeing the doctor that George had bought in. He looked very pleased with himself.

"Gents, ladies, I can announce that I am one hundred percent fit." He exclaimed. "Your doctor, George, reckons that I'll live for many years yet. So you can't get rid of me that easily!"

"And neither would we want to, Jack," smiled George, "we have a lot of catching up to do. What do you say about coming to live with Mildred and myself up at Whitehaven?"

"Love to, George! One thing, though, I'll be coming

back here on a regular basis, just to make sure these young scallywags don't get into any mischief!"

The end.

ABOUT THE AUTHOR

Peter was born in 1954 within the central part of Birmingham where communal bomb shelters and cobbled roads were the norm. Being the fifth of twelve children he has battled the scourge of losing his eyesight when he was just 29 years old but he has developed a mind of positive'ness that see's the creative side of his happy personality.

He worked as a qualified gardener for the local authority until he turned his hand to writing. This spiritualist has had many adventures of his own but the main part of his life has been dominated by episodes of the paranormal. Totally blind and still creating things within his beloved garden and home, he has a very natural sense of the spirit world.

He is guided by an intuitive spiritual force that see's him serving as a, 'Spiritual Healer' in his local community.

Lightning Source UK Ltd.
Milton Keynes UK
01 April 2010

152239UK00001B/10/P